Micah's Match

Lynn Howard

ISBN-978-1-949447-14-9
Micah's Match
Copyright @ 2019 by Lynn Howard

ALL RIGHTS RESERVED: No part of this book may be reproduced, stored in a retrieval system, or transmitted, in any form or by any means, without the prior permission in writing of the publisher, nor be otherwise circulated in any form of binding or cover other than that in which it is published and without a similar condition including this condition being imposed on the subsequent purchaser. Your non-refundable purchase allows you to one legal copy of this work for your own personal use. You do not have resell or distribution rights without the prior written permission of both the publisher and copyright owner of this book. This book cannot be copied in any format, sold, or otherwise transferred from your computer to another through upload, or for a fee.

Disclaimer: This book may contain explicit sexual content, graphic, adult language, and situations that some readers may find objectionable. This e-book is for sale to adults ONLY, as defined by the laws of the country in which you made your purchase. Lynn Howard will not be responsible for any loss, harm, injury or death resulting from use of the information contained in any of its titles.

This is a work of fiction. All characters, places, businesses, and incidents are from the author's imagination. Any resemblance to actual places, people, or events is purely coincidental. Any trademarks mentioned herein are not authorized by the trademark owners and do not in any way mean the work is sponsored by or associated with the trademark owners. Any trademarks used are specifically in a descriptive capacity.

Chapter One

She was so close. Callie had just a few more miles and she'd be in Big River Pack territory. She just hoped she'd find the refuge she sought and they didn't send her back to Tammen Pride.

Headlights were getting closer…and closer. Holy crap. That car was going way too fast and was going to hit her if they didn't slow down. When their bumper slammed into her rear, she realized it was intentional. She screamed when they hit her again and her car fishtailed. If she lost control of the car, they'd be on her faster than she could get out and run.

Callie leaned forward and squinted. There was too much fog and she could barely make out the road signs. There. Just ahead was the road leading to the Big River Pack.

Pushing her foot harder on the gas pedal, she continuously glanced in the rearview mirror at the assholes following her. Almost there. Almost.

The second the small homes came into view, Callie laid on her horn, praying the Pack would at least come outside to investigate the noise. She prayed even harder that they wouldn't turn their backs on her simply because she was a lioness.

"Come on! Get outside! There are people on your property! Where are you guys?" she yelled in the quiet of her car.

The Pride members who'd been chasing her hadn't slowed at all. They had no fear of Gray and his Pack. And as far as she could tell by all the vehicles parked out front, they were all there.

Callie didn't slow down until her car was almost to the first house. She slammed on her brakes and managed to plow over some lawn chairs and a firepit. The thud of the bricks hitting her car made her wince. That was definitely going to leave a dent.

The other car had stopped further back, but she still didn't dare climb out of her vehicle. Not until she spotted everyone on the front porches and climbing down their steps, angry scowls etched deep on their faces. The guy closest to her looked like he wanted to put his hand through her window until he bent a little and spotted her. A look of surprise widened his eyes, but did nothing for the deep furrow of his brows.

Pushing her door open, Callie realized how heavily she was breathing. Too much anxiety and fear had her heart racing as if she'd run a few miles. "Help," she breathed out, taking a step closer to where three males and a female stood.

She glanced up to see Gray and his mate on their porch. He pulled the woman with the rounded belly behind him and growled at the lion Shifters who'd climbed out of their truck and was stalking toward her.

"She's ours," Trever, the Second in the Tammen Pride, said.

"Doesn't look like she feels the same way," the pissed off guy at her back said. She turned and looked up at him. She'd never met any of this Pack; had never been allowed to leave the Pride Territory. But from the power rolling from him, she'd guess him as the Second in the Pack, Micah.

"Callie has a mate. She's to be returned to him immediately," Trever said.

"Whose orders?" Micah said, crossing his arms over his chest, making him appear even larger.

"Rhett," Eli said, but there was a hesitation in his answer. Eli was a good guy, but he was also a good soldier. While he might not agree with Rhett's orders, he also never fought them.

"You're in Big River territory now. If there any orders, they come from me. If your Alpha has an issue with that, tell him to call me," Gray said from his spot on the porch. He didn't come closer as if he didn't want to leave his mate unprotected.

"You really want that kind of war, Gray?" Trever said.

"We could just kill you now," Micah threatened.

Had he moved closer to Callie? He seemed to be almost hovering over her now, his dominance pressing on her lungs with too much pressure. But at the same time, she relished it, was intoxicated by it. She'd always hated being around dominant Shifters, but there was something different about this male.

"Or *we* could just kill *you*."

Callie's mouth popped open at how arrogant and stupid Trever was. Really? He thought the two of them could take on six wolves? Well, five; she knew the pregnant female couldn't Shift.

Micah took a step toward Trever, a terrifying smile on his face. He looked like he wanted the fight, like the thought excited him.

"Rhett's going to be pissed," Eli said, but he wrapped a hand around Trever's bicep and was pulling him backward.

"He knows where to find me," Gray said. "Time to go."

Callie turned and watched as Trever took a few steps in her direction. Eli pulled him back harder. "Not worth dying over tonight, Trever."

As the two men left, she realized she was left with these strangers. She didn't know them, didn't know if they'd kill her, didn't know anything about them. But when Micah turned and looked down at her, his eyes a bright blue, her heart stuttered in her chest and something felt like it had been tied between them, pulling her to him.

He took a step toward her, opened his mouth to say something, but his eyes widened. "You–"

"Does this mean we now have three chicks in our Pack?" a blonde guy asked as he sauntered over to where Callie and Micah were in a staring contest.

She glanced at him, then did a double take. He was naked as the day he was born. She looked down at his crotch, then looked away quickly, turning her entire body on him. "You mind putting on some pants?" she asked.

"Hey, I was in bed when you came racing in here like a crazy person. Sorry I didn't bother pulling on pajamas before hurrying out to rescue you."

Callie rolled her eyes, but then smiled when a small female grinned and shook her head.

"That's Reed. I'm Emory. That's Tristan over there," she pointed to a male who'd just stood by silently the whole time. "You already know Gray and his mate, Nova. And the weirdo standing behind you staring is Micah." Emory frowned at Micah like he'd lost his mind. "And Reed's gone. You can look." She winked and turned, heading back into her own home.

Callie turned back around. Gray and his mate had come off their porch and were making their way to her.

"What are you doing here?" Gray asked.

Micah, however, was still standing there staring with an odd expression on his face.

"I need help," Callie said.

"Yeah. We kind of gathered that," the Alpha's mate, Nova, said with a smile. "With what? I assume it has something to do with forced copulation?"

Callie's brows just about hit her hairline. "Huh?"

"That jackass said you have a mate, but it doesn't seem like you're all too happy to rush back to him. Were you one of those unfortunate unmated females who got suckered into joining their Pride?" Nova asked, taking another step closer. But Gray pulled her back, keeping her slightly behind his body.

"I'm not here to hurt anyone," Callie told Gray. Her eyes dropped to Nova's round stomach. As happy as she was for the couple, the sight of the pregnancy just made more anxiety burn through her veins. "Look. I'm sorry I came here. But you guys were the closest and I wasn't sure where else to go. I honestly thought Trever would back off when he figured out where I was headed."

"That dickhead isn't the smartest in the bunch," Reed said as he descended his stairs, this time wearing sweatpants.

Callie snorted. "Yeah, no." She looked around at the men and woman staring at her. "This is stupid, but would you mind if I hang around while I figure out what to do? I can sleep in my car, but I don't want to leave yet. They won't come back tonight. At least, I don't think so."

"Do you have a mate?" Micah asked. She turned to look up at him. Damn he was big. He had at least a foot on her.

"No."

"Then why'd he say that?" he asked, taking another step closer.

Callie raised her shoulders. "Because none of us really have a choice. And, by the way, the proper term would be mates. Plural. I've never seen one woman with a single male."

Growls erupted around her. Micah took yet another step closer. He dragged the shoulder of her shirt down then turned her and raised her hair. He was looking for marks. "Did they hurt you?" His voice was no longer human sounding; he was fighting his wolf.

"Not in the way you think," she said, pulling away from him and straightening her shirt.

More growls. But Nova approached her and tilted Callie's head up with gentle fingers on her chin, hissing through her teeth when she spotted the fading bruises on her throat. Like she had with Micah, she jerked away. "Look, do you mind if I stay the night in your territory? I won't cause any problems. If they come back, I'll go somewhere else." Her eyes dropped to Nova's belly. No way would she risk something happening to the pup growing in there.

"Reed, can she stay in your shed tonight? I don't want her sleeping out here all night where we can't see her."

Shed? Callie looked at the houses lined up in a row. They looked like all the other small homes most Shifters stayed in. Well, except her stupid Pride. They always needed bigger houses so the males could keep an eye on all his lionesses. All their mates were always housed in one home.

"No," Micah said, a snarl in his voice. "She'll stay in mine."

Everyone, including Callie, looked at him with surprise. He was the last one she'd expected to offer up his home. He didn't exactly seem welcoming and had stared at her with an odd expression since she'd pulled in front of his house.

But with his words came instant purring from her lion. *Nope. Not even entertaining that.* She shushed her lion and locked her away to deal with the problem at hand. She didn't need to create any more trouble for herself or these people.

Someone cleared their throat, there was soft chuckling, then the sounds of steps moving away from them. And then it was just her and Micah.

"Why?" she asked barely above a whisper.

"I can't fucking stand the Tammen Pride," he said, crossing his arms over his broad chest again. His hair was so black it blended in with the night sky as she stepped closer and tilted her head back to look at him.

"I can stay out here. Or on your porch if it's just a revenge thing."

Micah closed the space between them, stepping into her bubble, and bent at the waist until his mouth was a breath from hers. She gasped and couldn't breathe. Okay. Was he just trying to get her to breed with him instead? And why couldn't she make her hands lift to push him away?

Just when she thought he'd kiss her, he inhaled sharply and stepped back. "Come on," he said, turning and stomping up his stairs, never looking back to see if she was following.

Well, crap. She glanced back at the car for a second. He wasn't overly sweet, but inside his home was way better than being cramped inside the car and waking at every sound, convinced Tammen had come back for her.

Dropping her head with a soft groan, she trekked up his stairs, her legs feeling a little too heavy, and closed the door behind her.

Micah leaned against the counter, watching her as she turned and looked at him. When he didn't say anything, she checked out his place. Other than some beige and green striped curtains, the place was bare of any personal touches. His home looked like someone had just moved in. "Did you just move here?" she asked, unsure of what else to say. He shook his head and kept watching her. "How long have you lived here?"

"Long time," he said.

Finally, after studying her long enough to make her fidget, he turned and pulled two beers from the fridge, holding one out to her.

"I can't drink that," she said.

His eyes darted to her belly and he took a step back. "I thought you said no one touched you." His words were laced with that snarl again and his eyes flashed brilliant blue. She'd always loved the wolves' eyes but had never been so close to one when they were angry.

"They didn't. I just don't want my senses dulled and let those jackasses sneak up on me."

His body physically sagged a second like he was relieved. He offered the beer to her again. "No one will sneak up on you here. No one will fucking touch you as long as you're in our territory."

She crossed the room and grabbed the beer, but he didn't release it immediately. Just zeroed those eyes on her for a moment. And she felt that odd pull she'd felt outside, like a belt was being wrapped around them and tightened.

He let go of the beer and she put some space between them before she made a fool of herself. The last thing she needed was to throw herself at the wolf and beg him to claim her. Although, that wasn't a terrible idea. At least then, she could tell the lions she was officially mated and they'd have to leave her alone.

But was Trever right? Would her being there start a war? Would Micah claiming her damn his entire Pack? They didn't need a fight when they had a pregnant female among them. It was too dangerous, and Nova couldn't Shift to protect herself. Someone would have to stay out of the fight to guard her, shorting them one soldier.

But these people didn't seem like the kind to think of themselves as soldiers. She doubted they called themselves enforcers or talked about ruling the area, either. They just seemed like they wanted to live their lives and die happy at a ripe old age.

"What?" he asked as he moved closer to her. He kept walking until the back of her legs hit the edge of his couch. She looked around; his entire space was one big room. Meaning he slept on his couch every night.

"What are you doing?" she asked, her voice coming out far too breathy.

"You're purring. What are you thinking about?"

"You claiming me," she blurted out, then squeezed her eyes shut when she realized she'd once again spoken her thoughts. That was part of what always got her slapped around, her inability to hold her tongue, no matter how scared she was.

Micah's eyes blazed brighter and she glanced down at the bulge growing in his pants. He didn't even try to hide it when he adjusted his boner. And, yeah, now she was getting wet.

She wished she could blame her behavior or her body's reaction on the alcohol, but she'd yet to actually take a sip of the beer.

"Would that protect you?" he asked, his voice deep and husky.

"I—" But no words came. She couldn't form a coherent thought or sentence. Instead, she stood there panting as Micah stepped into her space again. He took her beer from her hand and set it and his on the floor.

When he rose slowly, she heard him scenting her. He could smell her arousal. "You know we have to fuck to claim a female, don't you?"

Oh, that sounded good. That sounded so good. But...

She ran away from her Pride because that was all they wanted from her. Was she ready to spread her legs for this stranger just to win his protection?

"Is that the only way you'll keep me safe?" she asked, but barely recognized her own voice.

He lifted his chin and looked down his nose at her. "You're safe as long as you're here. You owe me nothing. You owe us nothing."

And that just made her want him even more.

But he'd have to take her from behind. They didn't have to have sex for Micah to claim her in the way of her people, but her body warmed at the thought of him sliding in from behind while latching on. Lions claimed with a bite on the back of the neck. It was a carry-over from their wild ancestors.

As if she no longer had control over her body, Callie turned and raised her hair off her neck. Micah's arms encircled her waist and pulled her close until his erection was pressed against her ass. He might have been brutish, he might've seemed pissed that she'd woken him up with her chaos, but he definitely wanted her.

Her lion purred in her head and the sound escaped from her lips. Micah's lips were soft on her neck as he barely brushed them over her flesh, leaving soft kisses along the ridge there. She arched her back, pushing her ass into him further.

His lips parted and she felt the brush of teeth...

And then he gasped a deep inhale of breath and stepped away.

"What the fuck," he muttered as if to himself, as if he were confused. "What the fuck," he said louder.

She turned, her hand still holding her hair up, and looked at him with her brows pulled together. The scowl on his face made her drop her hair. What the hell had she been thinking? She'd just about begged him to take her right there against his counter. She'd practically begged him to mark her, to mate her. He wasn't her fucking mate…was he?

"I can't," he barked out, stomped past her, and yanked his door open. "That's the bed." He pointed to the couch. "Yell if you need me." Then he slammed the door and left her standing there, reeling.

What the fuck was right. That had been far too intense. And scary. She felt like she was in heat, but she had another week or two before that would happen. She needed to be gone before then.

And now that she was alone, she searched for her lioness deep inside. She was still purring away like crazy, but Callie knew that had all been her doing. Maybe Callie hadn't yet recognized Micah as her mate…but her lion had.

∞ ∞ ∞

Micah stood outside his door and pushed both hands through his hair. What the fuck? What the fuck had just happened? He knew what almost happened, but he had no idea how it had gotten to that point. Yeah, she was hot. She wasn't much taller than Emory, or as curvy as Nova, but she was drop-dead gorgeous. No wonder those Tammen fucks wanted her. She had a small waist, wide hips perfect for birthing cubs, and tits that would fill his hands.

Her blonde hair had been a little wild when she'd climbed out of her car, begging for help, but she'd constantly smoothed her hand over it like she was self-consciously grooming. Her every movement was smooth and graceful like the cat she was. Her eyes were the gold-brown of her people, but hers held tiny specks of green in them.

The fact he'd even noticed that pissed him off and he had the urge to put his fist through the wall separating him from Callie. But he wouldn't scare her like that. He'd let her rest knowing she was safe, and then tomorrow, he'd call one of his buddies and send her to the Ravenwood Pride for safekeeping.

Callie, his animal howled in his mind.

Micah gripped the sides of his head in both hands and squeezed. His fucking beast never shut up. Nova used to think he was always snarling at her, that he hated her. No. He hated himself. He hated his fucking animal.

And because of his messed up wolf, he'd almost claimed a lioness as his mate. That would've gone over just grand, especially when Tammen came looking for her again. And after being so close to her, after having her in his arms even for such a short period of time, he knew those fuckers would definitely be back. He'd tear through anyone and anything to get her back if she were his.

Sitting heavily onto the chair on his porch, he leaned forward and rested his elbows on his knees. He'd seriously almost fucked her, had almost sank his teeth into her neck. He didn't want a mate. Didn't need one. No; *she* didn't need *him*. He'd do nothing but screw up her life. It seemed like he did nothing but piss people off lately, even his own Pack. Hell, him and Gray fought at least once a week, and it was no longer over the Alpha's possessiveness of his mate.

Although now that he'd met Callie, he could almost understand…

What? What the hell was he thinking? No. Again, not *him*. His fucking crazy wolf. No matter how hard he tried, no matter how good of an act he put on, his wolf took over his actions more than was healthy.

Sniffling inside met his ears. Leaning to the side and peering through the window, he spotted Callie curled up on his couch, her arms wrapped around her knees, her face buried. She was crying. Had he made her cry? Was she crying out of relief? Fear?

Too many thoughts and emotions flooded him, the strongest was the urge to rip the door from its hinges and take her into his arms. He wanted to kiss her, to take away all her fear, to make her feel safe, cared for, to make her feel like she belonged.

But she didn't belong. She'd never be fully safe as long as she was there, especially in his house. Oh, she was safe from Tammen, but she'd never be safe from Micah.

As if she could feel his eyes on her, she lifted her head. Micah ducked into the shadows so he could continue to watch her without being seen.

Like a resolve came over her, she roughly wiped her tears away with the palms of her hands and stood. And Micah watched like a perv as she pulled her shirt over her head, unclasped her bra, and folded them both. She pushed her pants down next, but left on her white, cotton panties. She folded the pants and set all her clothes in a neat pile next to the couch, yanked the blanket off the back of the couch, and rolled over to her side.

He'd wanted her to stand there longer so he could admire her body some more. He'd thought she was hot in her jeans and t-shirt. That was nothing compared to her naked. His hands itched to trail over every inch of her body. He wanted to run his tongue from her toes to those perky tits. He wanted to taste every part of her.

Anger rushed him until he realized those weren't his wolf's thoughts or desires.

Those were all Micah. He wanted Callie. He wanted her in a way he'd never wanted anything or anyone.

Chapter Two

Callie rolled over and grunted. The couch wasn't much more comfortable than her car would've been. But she'd been safe and warm in Micah's home.

Memories of the night before had her sitting straight up as humiliation hit her hard and fast. She'd thrown herself at the Second of the Big River Pack last night. What had she been thinking? They weren't even the same species, for crying out loud. No wonder he'd run out when he realized what she'd been asking.

That wasn't true. He'd been pretty into her at first. Maybe she hadn't seen it or touched it yet, but she could tell by the way he pushed against her that Micah was packing a pretty big gun in those worn out jeans.

And then she realized she'd said *yet*. She hadn't touched him *yet*.

Dropping back onto the couch, she pulled the blanket up further so her breasts were covered. There was a soft tap on the door. Callie turned her head and looked through the glass. Micah was standing on his own porch, knocking on his own door, asking permission to come into his own damn house.

Reaching down, she quickly pulled on her t-shirt, then padded over to the door. "What are you doing? It's your house, Micah." She smiled up at him, but he didn't return the smile.

"You were naked. I didn't want to embarrass you."

She frowned at him. "How did you know I was naked?"

A sheepish half-smile pulled up the corners of his lips as he pointed at the window beside the door.

"You watched me take off my clothes last night?" She tried her hardest to be mad, but, instead, found herself turned on.

He shrugged. "I said I'd keep you safe. I didn't say anything about being a gentleman with a beautiful woman in my house."

He'd called her beautiful. She wasn't naïve. She knew her looks were why Tammen wanted to breed her so badly. She'd give them strong cubs. It was the same reason Deathport wanted their small female, Emory. She was pretty and strong. And unmated.

Micah's eyes dropped to her bare legs peeking out from her t-shirt. It barely covered her undies. She quickly grabbed her pants from the ground and hoped Micah had averted his eyes when she'd undoubtedly flashed him a glimpse of the white cotton. Then again, he'd already admitted to being a voyeur last night.

When she pulled her jeans up her legs and over her ass, she caught his eyes following the motion. Heat bloomed low in her belly, but she stifled it. They'd almost gotten carried away last night and done something really stupid. With all his Pack awake, she didn't need to risk them hearing her riding him like a rabid cowgirl.

And there she was again, fantasizing about this man taking her, marking her as his.

"Alpha wants to talk to you," Micah said, but she heard the huskiness in his voice. And, yep, he was sporting yet another impressive boner.

"About what?"

"I assume what we're going to do with you," Micah said, leading her out of his house.

Fear burned her gut at that thought. *What they were going to do with her.* She'd never heard of Big River being cruel. Hell, they had an unmated female living right smack in the middle of them and no one had forced anything on her.

Gray, Nova, Tristan, and Emory all sat in the chairs she hadn't ruined last night.

"Any chance you're good with stone work?" Reed asked as they approached.

He was attempting to rebuild the ruined firepit and winked at her when she apologized. She couldn't even offer to buy another one or pay someone to repair it. Lionesses weren't allowed to work, weren't allowed to have their own money. Hell, they weren't even allowed to live alone. She wasn't even supposed to be driving, but it wasn't her fault one of the males had left his keys in the ignition.

"What are your plans?" Gray asked as he gestured to one of the open chairs. Micah didn't sit, but he did stand pretty close to her. Gray didn't miss it. His eyes moved to Micah, a slight frown formed between his brows, but then he returned his attention to Callie.

"I honestly don't know. I've never met anyone from Ravenwood. Do they force females into breeding?" Ravenwood was a Pride full of panther Shifters, but at least they were of the feline genes like her.

"Fuck, no," Reed said. "We wouldn't be friends with them if they did."

"How come the council hasn't done anything about all that?" Nova asked Gray.

He inhaled and exhaled through his nose. "It's an old antiquated law that says any Shifter has the right to claim and breed an unmated female. Pretty sure there's nothing in there about forcing a woman, but there are always loopholes."

"Can't you talk to your dad?" Emory asked Nova.

"I called him and left a voicemail. I'll see if there's anything he can do."

"Your dad?" Callie asked, confused by the conversation.

"I just met my dad last year. Turns out he's a member of the council. Pretty cool, right?"

Callie smiled at her. She couldn't help herself. All the females in her Pride were either broken and shut down or ruthless and wanted nothing to do with the lower level breeders. And there was no other way to think of the women than as breeders. A majority of them didn't have a true mate and really didn't want to be there, but, like Callie, didn't know where else to go.

"Could you ask Ravenwood if I'd be welcome there?"

"Just stay here," Micah said. Everyone turned wide eyes on him, including Callie. "You're just as safe here as you would be there. They don't have any open homes, either. And none of us would ever force anything on you."

Yeah, but she'd almost forced something on him last night. She feared if she stayed there too long, if she stayed near Micah, things would get out of hand.

But when everyone turned those wide eyes on her and smiled, she figured she didn't really have anything else to lose. Not that she had anything to lose before. Except her sanity and her...

Shit. She hadn't even mentioned her sexual inexperience to Micah when she'd begged him to take her last night.

Once again, she was obsessing over the wolf behind her instead of worrying about her own safety. But he could keep her safe. He'd promised her. More or less.

"If I stay here, will it cause problems for you guys?" she asked, shifting in her seat.

"Yes—"

"No—" Gray and Nova said at the same time.

"We don't need those assholes showing up here again with you being pregnant."

"So, we get ahold of Ravenwood and Blackwater. Let them know what's going on. They won't let anyone mess with us."

"They don't live here," Gray said, taking his mate's hand. "It would take too long for them—"

"Oh, bull crap. It takes them ten minutes to get here when you tell them we're grilling. I swear it's even less than that when you tell them we're providing the beer. You call them or I will. If she wants to stay here, she's staying. Micah, can she keep staying in your shed until we can get her her own?"

Why did she keep calling their houses sheds? She was odd and outspoken, but Callie really liked her. Emory was smiling at her, too, probably excited about having another female around.

"Great, another chick in the territory. This is going to be fun when they all sync up," Reed grumbled. All eyes turned to him. "Their periods," he explained.

"How do you know about that?" Emory asked, the widest grin on her face.

"Unlike you boring people, I actually watch TV quite often. They said something about it on one of those talk shows."

"You're watching talk shows now, too?" Emory asked, winking over at Callie.

Her Pride had never joked and played like this. Never. Well, the men might have, but never around the lionesses. And those females definitely never played.

As she listened to the banter, she found herself relaxing, something she hadn't done since she'd been brought to Tammen at sixteen. They'd told her parents they wouldn't mate with her until her twenty-first birthday, but they'd tried from day one. She was twenty-two now and the male chosen for her was growing impatient. It was getting harder and harder to fight him off.

"Callie!" Nova called out, snapping her fingers. "You cool, girl? You look like you kind of zoned out there for a second."

Callie looked around to find everyone staring at her with looks varying from confused to amused. And she realized she'd totally just rhymed in her head.

With a shy smile, she nodded. "Yeah. Sorry. I was just thinking."

"About staying?" Nova said with a big smile, drawing out each word.

Once again, Callie looked to each face, searching for the answer. No one looked pissed at the idea, but Tristan, the quiet one who she'd yet to hear actually speak, looked a little worried. Glancing over her shoulder, she found Micah watching her closely. When he nodded his head once, she had her answer.

"Yeah. I'll stay until I figure something else out."

"Yay!" Nova blurted out and clapped her hands. "Okay. We've got to go shopping. You'll need your own shed, a bed, some cooking stuff...oh my gosh, this is almost as much fun as shopping for Wolfgang."

Callie looked around, confused. "Who's Wolfgang?"

"We don't know what we're having, boy or girl, so that's what I nicknamed our little puppy."

"Dude! Stop calling him a puppy. He's not a dog," Reed said, wrapping his hand around his forehead and rubbing his temples with his thumb and fingers.

"Hey, he's part wolf, just like his momma and daddy. And he...or *she* is mine. I'll call *her* whatever I want."

"Gray? You're not going to stop her?" Reed asked, throwing his hands out toward Nova in frustration.

The Alpha just smiled and shook his head. The lionesses never got to name their own cubs. They could suggest names, but that didn't mean their male would accept it. These people reminded her more of a human family than a Shifter group. Although, her birth Pride and the one she'd been pawned off on were the only ones she'd ever known. Maybe the rest of the Shifters were like this group, loving and kind and ready to risk their own safety for a stranger.

"Do you have any names picked out?" Callie asked, then ducked her eyes for a second. What an intimate question to ask.

But Nova made a hiss sound at her. When Callie looked up, Nova was shaking her head slowly. "No more looking down, kitty cat. Just because you were born with a vagina, doesn't mean you're beneath anyone."

"I really wish you wouldn't say vagina," Reed groaned.

"Would you rather I say coochie? No? How about hooha…twat?"

"Oh my gawwwd! Gray, please put something in her mouth to shut her up," Reed said, then his eyes went wide. "Dude, don't kill me. I totally meant food. I don't have a dirty mind like your little woman there."

Callie hadn't really found anything Nova said dirty. Funny, absolutely. She frowned and smiled slightly in confusion.

"I'm a romance author. I write about love and sex. A lot of sex," she explained.

The author. That was right. Gray had mated with the woman Deathport had been after. They'd been so pissed when she'd mated with Gray so quickly and they'd lost their chance. She'd overheard the Alphas of her Pride and Deathport making plans of how they were going to take down Big River. In the end, though, Big River had come out fine and Anson, Deathport's Alpha, had been warned by the council. She'd loved that news.

"Back to the fun stuff. When do you want to go shopping? Reed can come with us. Or Micah."

"Or all of us. Two unmated females and a pregnant mate? Nope." Gray put his hands in front of him when Nova whirled on him. "Sorry, princess. Not risking my mate *or* my daughter."

"Ha! See? He thinks it's a girl, too," Nova said to Reed before sticking her tongue out at him.

Callie's cheeks went warm with embarrassment. "I can't. I don't have any money."

"Oh, please. I have plenty of money. My new book exploded. Ladies can't get enough of horny country boys."

Gray leaned over and pressed his lips to hers in a public show of affection…something else she'd never seen.

"I can't let you do that," Callie said.

A warm hand landed on her shoulder and all eyes zeroed right in on that hand. Callie looked to her left to find Micah standing beside her. "You can stay in my place until you get your own."

"So you can sleep on the porch and play peeping Tom again?" she teased, but didn't miss the flash of heat in his eyes, nor the way his gaze dipped to her chest before raising back to her face.

"You were totally watching her through the window last night, weren't you, perv?" Reed said. Micah glared at him until he held his hands up and sat back in his chair.

"It's fine, guys. Seriously. I've been wanting the chance to build another shed and design it and all that fun stuff. And this one will be pretty like Emory's," Nova said, her infectious smile wide.

"You made ours pretty," Gray argued.

"Yeah, but this will be just hers. There won't be any big, muddy shoes sitting in the middle of the living room or dirty dishes in the sink," Nova said, cocking an eyebrow at Gray. Just like Reed had done, he raised his hands in surrender and sat back. "What do you say? Want to go shopping?"

"I don't know," Callie said, looking up at Micah again.

"Okay. How about this? We'll call it temporary. It'll be yours as long as you want it, and if you decide to leave, it can be a guest house or even a play area for Wolfgang."

That didn't sound as bad as when Nova outright said she wanted to buy Callie a house. If she stayed there long enough, she could get her first job and pay Nova back. Eventually. She had no idea how she'd pay the entire Pack back for their kindness, for taking her in when they knew danger followed her. But, somehow, she'd find a way.

∞ ∞ ∞

When Callie agreed to stay in their territory, just a couple houses down from his own, Micah had the insane urge to pick Nova up and hug her. But he wouldn't. Not only did he not show affection, ever, but he didn't want to fight Gray in front of Callie.

Instead of hugging anyone, he grunted and volunteered to ride along with the women. He didn't have to. They all piled into a couple of trucks and went to the store as one big fucking family.

He'd somehow managed to corral Emory and Callie in his truck, although he'd rather have been alone with Callie. Which was stupid. He was already fighting his animal and his libido to stay away from her when all he wanted to do was pull her across the cab, drag her onto his lap, and kiss her until she was lust drunk.

So, he turned up the radio to drown out his thoughts before he embarrassed himself and Callie and got them all in a shit load of trouble.

But maybe Callie had had a point last night. Maybe if Micah claimed her, the Tammen Pride would leave her alone. It might cause an even bigger riff between the Pride and his Pack, but he didn't fucking care. He hated them all. They were nothing but a bunch of power hungry, woman using assholes.

Callie stayed pretty closed off the entire drive into Fenton. Emory got tired of the silence and leaned forward, resting her elbows on the backs of their seats. "Can you turn that down?" she yelled over the music. Micah sneered at her over his shoulder, but turned the knob, making the music more of a background noise rather than a thought cancelling crutch. "Hey, Callie. How long were you with Tammen?"

Finally unfolding her arms from around her stomach, she turned her upper half to look at Emory. "Since I was sixteen. Six years."

"You were able to stay unpregnant for six years?"

"Unpregnant isn't a word," Micah said. His tone was chastising, but he was struggling to keep his anger at bay. The mere mention of someone touching Callie, especially against her will, made Micah want to hunt down every member of that Pride and eviscerate them.

"She knew what I meant. Go back to being mopey and let the girls talk." Emory turned her attention back to Callie. "Well? Are you just a total badass or something?"

Callie snorted. "No. Well, maybe a little."

"You seriously *fought* fought them?" Emory said, her voice rising an octave.

"When I had to," Callie said.

Micah glanced at her as she shoved her thumb into her mouth to chew the skin around her nail. He could tell she was growing uncomfortable with the conversation. Micah opened his mouth to warn Emory, to tell her to back off, but Callie beat him to it.

"Can we talk about something else?" she blurted out.

"Of course. Let's talk about what you're going to do with your house," Emory said with a bright smile. Emory had her own secrets. She knew when it was time to drop something.

"Oh. I don't know. I've never done anything like this. Is Nova seriously going to pay for everything?"

"Yes," both Micah and Emory said. Micah rolled his eyes, but Emory smiled.

"You'll get used to it. She loves to buy gifts for everyone. Sometimes it's something small like a houseplant or an ornament around Christmas time. She bought the Pack a killer grill and that fire pit. I'll bet she's excited as hell you broke it so she can buy another one. I think her love language is gifts."

"Love language?" Micah grumbled. He'd wanted to be around Callie, to spend time with her, but he didn't know if he could handle the chick talk.

"It's a known fact everyone has a love language. Gray's is more physical. That's why he never turns down a fight and always pats us on the back or squeezes our shoulders. Reed and I are more verbal. We just say what we're thinking. Yours? I'm still trying to figure out your love language. Oh, I know. Food. You always end up being the one to cook for us. That's got to be it."

"I don't have a love language," he grumbled as he pulled in behind Gray's truck.

They all lined up beside the storage sheds outside the hardware store. Nova was obsessed with these even though they'd told her over and over they'd all built theirs, not gone to the damn store and picked one out.

But Callie couldn't build herself a home. And he doubted she'd stay in his house much longer after he admitted to watching her get naked. Almost naked. Not quite naked enough.

This time, he could tell when his wolf was pushing ahead harder and shoved him back just as hard. *Not now. Fuck off.*

Callie, his wolf whined as she walked ahead of him with Emory and Nova flanking each side. Her tight little ass swayed with each step. Did she even realize how fucking sexy her walk was? Micah stopped and searched inwardly; nope, that wasn't his wolf that time. Great. He was going even crazier and this woman was sending him on a downward spiral.

"What about this one? We can get some stuff and make it bigger," Nova asked as she stroked her belly in circles.

"We?" Reed and Gray asked.

"Yeah, we, as in you big, strong men. Hey, don't look at me. I'm in a delicate state, remember?" She hugged her belly so it was more prominent.

Gray's face softened and even Reed shuffled his feet. Those idiots would do anything for Nova. Who was he kidding? He might not make it obvious, but he always made sure to get her favorites when it was his turn to buy the food for the cookouts. He was secretly excited to have a pup in the Pack.

Callie.

Oh, for fuck's sake. All it took was him thinking about kids and his wolf started pining for the woman looking back at him for his opinion.

"Yeah. We can make it better," he said with a shrug, faking for all he was worth that he didn't care either way.

She smiled at him and his heart fluttered. Again, he searched for his wolf, but that was all Micah. The longer she stayed near him, the more fucked he realized he was.

The women picked Callie's house and then they all filed in to get the rest of the supplies. While Reed and Tristan headed deeper into the store for the lumber and plumbing needs, Micah and Gray stayed with the females as they picked out Callie's curtains, her sinks, her shower fixtures, even her fucking toilet.

"Okay. This is all too much," Callie said a little breathlessly as she took in the four carts they wheeled to the checkout lane.

"No it's not. We still got to get you dishes and cookware. We're not done shopping yet," Nova said with a whole lot of excitement. The woman was practically glowing. He'd never met anyone who gained so much joy simply from buying other people shit.

"Oh, wait." Emory turned and looked down the rows. "What about houseplants?"

"Yeah. Definitely need—"

"No more," Callie said with a huffy laugh. "Seriously. It's going to take me forever to pay you back for all of this."

"I told you, just live there as long as you want and then we'll use it for something else. Oooooh, a She-Shed," Nova said, looking to Emory with wide eyes.

"Isn't that what you call my house?" Emory said.

Micah tuned them out and studied Callie. While the two of them were having the time of their lives, they didn't notice how pale Callie was growing. She was scared. Or anxious. Or both. "I'll get her dishes," Micah said, cutting off whatever ridiculous thing they were discussing now.

"What?" Callie said, turning to look up at him.

"I'll get them, and if you leave," he said and prayed it was a major *if* and not *when*, "I'll just take the new stuff and put my old stuff in there. It's a win-win. No more arguing. Let's go."

He took the cart Nova was pushing and shoved it toward where Tristan and Reed were waiting.

"Micah," Gray called out. He didn't slow as his Alpha jogged to catch up. "You cool, brother?"

"I'm fine. She's not," he said, jerking his thumb over his shoulder.

Gray looked behind them. "Nova's fine. She ate in the truck and–"

But Micah cut him off. "Not Nova. Callie. This is a lot for her. You heard her back at home. The women weren't allowed anything of their own. No job. No money. No home. All this shit is overwhelming her."

He probably should've lowered his voice, but even if he'd whispered, everyone would've heard him anyway. At least this way, Callie didn't have to be the one to tell everyone to chill the fuck out.

After everything was loaded up in the trucks, Emory climbed in with Reed while Callie rode with Micah again. There were about twenty minutes of silence before Callie reached forward and turned the music down. "Thanks for that back there," she said softly.

He glanced at her then turned his eyes back to the road. "You've got to speak up for yourself or those girls will have you blowing money on shit like chandeliers." He knew what she meant, but gave her an out. She didn't need to thank him. He'd have done it for any of his Pack. She might not be one of theirs yet, but that didn't mean he wouldn't protect her from everything, including overzealous new girlfriends.

Shit. He'd said *yet*. She wasn't a part of his Pack *yet*. Even as he tried to argue with himself and his wolf, he realized he was losing the war. He'd already lost the battle the second he'd felt her pushed up against his hard body.

Chapter Three

Callie borrowed a pair of shorts and a tank top from Emory and went to work unloading everything. The shed they'd chosen would be there within the hour and they wanted to be ready to get to work. They'd have to tap into Tristan's power and plumbing, but the quiet fucker didn't mind. Just shrugged and nodded when they'd asked if it was okay.

Micah was one of the three people in his Pack who didn't know Tristan or Emory's background. That was fine; none of them knew a thing about his. And he planned on keeping it that way. It was none of their business and had nothing to do with them.

Retreating to his house, Micah headed straight for the bathroom and leaned over the sink. He stared at his reflection in the mirror, wondering who the hell he'd become. He'd just met this chick and already, he was tempted to tell her everything about himself in hopes of winning her over and earning her trust.

He splashed water on his face and neck and straightened when he heard his front door open and close. Glancing around the curtain separating the bathroom from the rest of the house, he froze when he spotted Callie standing there with a sheen of sweat on her face and chest. He didn't even need to question which side of him was in control when he had the urge to lick every drop of dew from her skin. That was all Micah.

"What's up?" he asked, trying to act cool.

"Do you mind if I grab a bottle of water?" she asked, wringing her hands in front of her. She had no problem speaking her mind, but was scared to ask for something as simple as water?

"You don't have to ask for anything, Callie. Just get in there and take what you want. You hungry?"

"Not really," she said, her eyes dipping to the floor before raising to his face. Already, he was learning her tells. She was hungry. She'd fought those bastards off her body, but they'd done a number on her mind.

Drying his face, he tossed the towel into the hamper and made a beeline for the fridge. Instead of making a meal and spending time they didn't have since the shed would be there soon, he pulled some leftover hot dogs from the fridge and popped them in the microwave.

"You don't have to do that," she said, but her eyes were on the microwave. Shit. She hadn't eaten before they left and they hadn't stopped for anything. When was the last opportunity she'd had to fill her belly?

"I want to," he said, setting the plate in front of her and turning to grab the buns from the top of his fridge. When he turned around, she already had one in her mouth. The sight of her slipping that stupid fucking hot dog between her lips made his dick jump. "Here," he said a little more gruffly than he'd intended. He pulled a couple of buns out and shoved the hot dogs in the middle. "Ketchup?"

"Mustard, please," she said around a mouthful, and he had to stifle a moan when her little pink tongue darted out to lick her bottom lip.

He grabbed the mustard, set it in front of her, then turned for the door. "Just come out when you're finished. Take your time." He couldn't stay in there and watch her eat with the fantasies of sliding his cock between her lips playing in his mind.

Fuuuck. And that was definitely all Micah, none of his wolf.

Twenty minutes later, a big semi came grumbling down the road with her new place on the trailer. She stepped outside and his heart warmed at the smile on her face. "You ready?" he asked as he led her down the stairs.

"I still can't believe this is happening," she said, but it was more to herself than Micah.

Emory and Nova swarmed her, talking her ear off about the slumber parties they were going to have and how pretty her place would be when they were done.

"Shoot," Nova said, stomping her food. "We forgot paint."

"It's fine, Nova. Really," Callie said, but her eyes were glued on that little shack as it got towed to the end of the row of houses.

It took them three days to get her place ready for her to move in, and Micah was about to go blind with how much he'd jerked off in the shower while having her in his place every night. The first night, he'd slept on the porch again. But by the second night, Callie had demanded he come in.

"You've already seen me practically naked. Might as well just sleep in here with me."

But he couldn't make her give up the couch. He'd just spread out on the floor, accepting a couch cushion she'd passed down. Nova had loaned them a few extra blankets, so he'd used one as some padding between him and the floor and the other to hide his boner every night. He knew she wasn't stupid and noticed the tent he made the second she climbed under her own blanket and pulled off her clothes.

Her place was great, but Nova was right. It definitely needed some paint. The walls were raw wood and he worried she'd get a splinter if she rubbed up against it. And then he felt like punching himself in the dick for worrying about something so minor.

But he was in deep already. No matter how hard he fought, he couldn't keep his thoughts or eyes off the graceful lioness living two doors down from him.

He'd hated the day she moved into her place and left his. He'd tried to get her to wait while they applied dry wall and paint, but she wouldn't. He understood. This was the first time in her twenty-two years she had full control of her own life. She was free to come and go as she pleased at Micah's, but that wasn't her own home.

That first night, he laid on his couch, surrounded by her scent, and stared up at the ceiling. He missed her. It was so fucking stupid, but he missed her. She was two houses down, but he fucking missed her.

After three hours of laying there wide awake, he pushed to his feet and wandered onto his porch. Everyone was asleep; their houses were all dark. There was no sound. But, down the row, there was a light on in Callie's house.

Looking to his right, he checked one more time that none of the rest of his Pack were up and could see him acting like a tool before stepping off his porch and hurrying to Callie's.

He stopped at the bottom step. What was he doing? This was her first night on her own and he was ready to ruin it. He needed to give her space. If she wanted him to visit, she'd let him know.

Backing away quietly, he froze when her front door opened. "Couldn't sleep?" she asked.

He turned and held his breath at the sight of her. Emory and Nova had taken her shopping for some clothes yesterday, but this time, Micah had demanded he pay for it. He hadn't realized how much chicks' clothes cost.

She stood framed by the door in nothing but a short ass pair of sleep shorts and a skimpy tank top. Even from there, he could see her nipples pebbled and straining against the thin cotton. Wasn't cold outside. He smiled inwardly with pride; her body was reacting to him.

"Want to come in?" she asked, her face hopeful.

He'd worried about ruining her first night in her first home, but she looked like she really didn't want him to say no. So he didn't.

"Yeah. Sure," he said, and had to restrain himself from sprinting up the stairs to be near her.

When did he become this person? When did he get so lost in another living creature? He'd shied from commitments, hid from attachments. But every single fiber of his being knew he'd lose what little sanity he had if this stunning woman walked out of his life for good.

She stepped out of the way to make room for him, and he was once again reminded of how petite she was. Not quite as small as Emory, but close to a foot shorter than himself. She watched him as he wandered the small space, nodding at the way she and the girls had decorated.

"It's nice," he said.

"I missed you," she blurted out, then sucked her lips into her mouth. "I shouldn't have said that."

He didn't recognize the person he'd become when Callie had come tearing into his life, but he didn't care. He crossed the space in two steps, wrapped his hand in her hair, and claimed her lips like he wanted to claim her body.

She gasped into his mouth and he took the opportunity to taste her. Sweet, like candy. Addictive. He needed more. Wrapping his other arm around her body, he pulled her closer. Instead of pushing him away, she wrapped her arms around his neck, pulling his hair with one hand.

As Micah lifted her, she wrapped her legs around his waist and writhed. She was like a cat in heat.

Pulling away with a start, he stared down into her eyes. Bright gold. She wasn't fully Callie right now. Just like he'd done constantly for the past week, she was fighting her animal for control.

"Callie," he said, his breath coming fast. She stared at him, her lips parted, her heart racing. "Are you sure about this?"

Her eyes slowly bled to their golden-brown color and she frowned. "Oh yeah," she said with an exaggerated nod. Then her eyes dipped for just a second before rising back to his. "I have to tell you something first."

He carried her to the futon and sat with her straddling his lap. "What? You said you weren't mated." *Please don't let that have been a lie*. He couldn't detect it on her, but maybe it was different with the whole interspecies thing. Maybe it wasn't such a deterrent.

"I've never..." She squeezed her eyes shut and dropped her head.

He watched her, confused, and then it dawned on him and he dropped his hands like she was hot metal. "Are you trying to say you're a...but you're twenty-two years old." She was a virgin? How was that fucking possible? She'd been with the Tammen Pride for six years and had remained a virgin? Then again, she'd said she'd fought them off any time they'd tried anything.

"Because I didn't want to lose it to someone who just wanted my ovaries. Well, I mean, of course they wanted more, too, but you get my point." She looked angry now. He liked the angry Callie more than the defeated Callie. She was even sexier with that fire in her eyes.

"You don't want me to be your first, Callie." He gripped her waist to pick her body up off his lap, but she settled in and crossed her arms.

"Would you hurt me?"

"No."

"Would you force me to do anything I don't want?"

"Fuck, no. You should know that by now."

She lowered her arms and rested one hand on his bare chest. "Do you want me?" Her voice was soft and husky.

His heart thundered behind his ribs, he couldn't catch his breath, and his balls were about to explode from stopping so close to the goal. Yeah, he wanted her. "If we do this, especially with you being a virgin, I don't know if I can stop myself from marking you." And then he realized he'd just basically admitted what he'd been trying to deny to himself.

"I've known you were my real mate since the day I saw you. There was something, this weird force that felt like we were tied together, and every time we walked away from each other, it felt like it was trying to pull me back. And my lioness won't leave me alone."

He huffed out a laugh. He knew all about psychotic inner animals.

"Do you *want* me to mark you?" he asked as his heart raced even harder, if that was at all possible. He never wanted this. Never. But with Callie, it felt like there was a weird hole deep inside of him that was finally filling by just having her in his life, in his home, in his arms.

She searched his eyes, her gaze bouncing between them. "I don't know. I mean, I do, but...it has to be from behind. I'm kind of scared."

Of course, she was. She was a fucking virgin. No way was he going to take her hard and fast from behind while sinking his fangs into her neck. Not for her first time.

With as much restraint as he could muster, he raised his hands and cupped her face. "Are you sure you want me to be your first, Callie? We don't have to do a fucking thing. I can sleep on the floor beside the couch just like before if you're scared to stay alone tonight."

"It's not that, Micah. I want to be with you. I'm not scared. I know all of you would hear if anyone tried to get into my house. But I really, truly missed you." Her eyes dipped to his chest. "That sounds really stupid, doesn't it?"

He forced her to look at him with a finger under her chin. "I missed you so fucking bad." He hated admitting that out loud and was glad there was no one else around to witness this moment of weakness, but she held zero judgement in her eyes. She didn't see him as a jerk or some asshole. She just saw *him*. She just saw Micah.

Closing the space between them, Callie touched her lips to his in the sweetest caress he'd ever experienced. Her hands slid up his bare chest to lock around the back of his neck. He pressed his hands flat on her back and pulled her closer until her perky little tits were smashed against his chest. Through the thin material of her sleep shirt, he could feel her hard nipples rub against him as her breathing increased.

Micah was trembling with the strength it took not to rip her clothes off, toss her onto the couch, and slide into her. She'd need him to be patient with her, take it slow, work her body until she was prepared for his size. Nothing scared him. Nothing. But he was terrified of hurting her.

Turning, he laid Callie back on the couch, never pulling his mouth from hers. He could seriously kiss her all night. But he needed more. She needed more. He just wasn't sure how much he could give her tonight. Had no one talked to her about the first time? The possibility of pain? She wanted him to be her first, but he wasn't sure he could put her through something like that.

Skimming his hand across her cheek, he let it wander down her throat to her shoulder then between the valley of her breasts. She moaned softly into his mouth and his dick grew harder; all blood flow had officially left his brain and settled in his crotch. At this rate, he'd have permanent imprints of his zipper on his shaft.

Callie pulled her mouth from his and turned her head to the side a little, as if begging for his teeth. Not yet. He needed her to feel good before he sank his fangs into her.

He took the opportunity to nip at her jawline, her throat, and her shoulders as he cupped one of her tits in his big hand. He squeezed and massaged, tweaking her nipple through her tank top. She moaned again and he thought he'd come in his pants from that throaty sound.

He needed to taste her. All of her. Micah kissed a path down her body, dragging the tank top up so he could wrap his lips around her dark pink nipple. She tangled her fingers in his hair and held him there, her back arching from the couch and pushing her chest into his face.

Moving slowly, he trailed his hand down her body, under her shorts, and past her panties. His fingers slid through her folds to find her wet for him. She spread her legs and writhed against his hand.

Fuuuck. His control was slipping quickly, and if she kept humping his hand like that, his control was going to blow the fuck up.

"Callie, slow down, kitty," he whispered against her chest. He followed his hand with his mouth, kissing and licking a path down her body. She kept her hands tangled in his hair. When he raised his eyes to her face, she was watching him with an unfocused look in her eyes as if she were as lost to the moment as he was.

Pulling his hand from her shorts, he hooked his fingers in the hips and peeled them and her skimpy panties down her thighs. He tossed them to the ground and settled between her thighs, kissing each before lowering his head. The first long swipe of his tongue and she threw her head back with another of those sexy moans. She was practically purring as he licked and sucked her clit.

Her heavy pants told him she was close. As gently as he could, he pushed a finger into her to the first knuckle. She gasped and tightened around him, so he stopped but kept working her with his mouth. He had to make this as easy for her as he could.

When Callie relaxed again and her breathing quickened, he pushed his finger in a little more, staying as slow as he physically could. His wolf was howling and pacing in his head, but Micah pushed him as far back in his mind as he could to focus on Callie, her needs, her pleasure.

"Micah," she breathed out.

He increased the pressure with his tongue and pushed his finger in a little more. He knew the instant he broke through. She tensed but her orgasm was building. He'd managed to time that shit perfectly. Pumping into her slowly, he continued to work her clit until she opened her mouth and released a long, low moan and her sex clenched around his finger.

He pulled from her and sucked her clit softly, helping her ride out the last of her aftershocks. After a few minutes, she lifted her head and looked down at him with a drunken smile. "Wow," she breathed out.

If his balls weren't turning blue, he'd have puffed up with manly pride. A glance down at his hand and he wanted to slam his dick in the door. Her blood was all over his finger and nail. He'd caused her to bleed.

Callie followed his eyes and shrugged. "I thought it'd been worse." She frowned down at him when his anger at himself didn't subside. "You did know that would happen, didn't you?"

"Yeah. But I still made you bleed."

She sat up clumsily and just smiled. "It's nothing, Micah. It's okay. You didn't hurt me." He just couldn't make the self-degradation go away. He'd never do anything to hurt her, and even though she kept trying to reassure him, he felt like the biggest asshole on the fucking planet. "Come here," she said, holding her arms open.

Micah wiped his finger on his jeans, cleaning the blood away. He lifted and moved so he was lying with his weight off her, just to the side. She wrapped her arms around his neck and tried to drag his mouth down to her.

"I can't," he growled out, fully aware how present his wolf was.

"Why not?" She trailed her hand slowly down his chest and flattened her palm against his hard length. "I think you definitely can."

"I don't want to hurt you again, Callie. I can't."

She stared up into his eyes and her smile faded. "It might hurt for a second, but I trust you, Micah. I trust you'll stop if it's too much. It always burns a little the first time. I was warned by the other lionesses a long time ago. I think that's partly why I always rejected Brent. He gets off on others' pain. He would've done everything he could to–"

Micah placed a hand over her mouth and stopped any more words. "Please. Don't say another word about him or I'll end up hunting the fucker down tonight."

And he would. The thought of that son of a bitch raping her, knowing she was a virgin, doing everything he could to cause her pain made his wolf thrash in his head. His vision was tinted on the outsides with red and he wasn't sure how much more restraint he had for the night.

"Sorry," she mumbled through his fingers.

"Don't fucking apologize. To anyone. Ever." He pulled his hand from her mouth.

She lifted her hand and cupped the side of his face. "I can't believe I actually found my mate," she whispered, her tone full of awe. He felt the same fucking way, although his was laced with a shit load of fear, mainly for her. "Does it suck that I'm not a wolf?"

"What? No. Why would it?"

"I'm not sure if I'd give you a pup or a cub," she admitted, then bit her bottom lip. "Too soon. Too soon to talk about that or even think about that."

It was too soon, but the fact she'd even thought about it flipped some primal switch inside of him. Dropping his head, he covered her mouth with his and drank her in. Her hands were on his face, his back, his chest. And then they were moving lower. She yanked at the button of his jeans and ripped the zipper down.

When her small hand slipped past the waist band and gripped his dick, he pulled from her mouth with a hiss. "Callie," he moaned. "I don't know if I can stop if you keep touching me—"

She silenced him with her lips. She stroked his length slowly, gripping him tighter. His hips bucked forward like they had a mind of their own. Her fingers left him and shoved at the waist of his pants, forcing them over his hips and exposing him fully. Even with his brain turning to mush, he had enough cells left to push off the couch and remove his pants. His wolf was silent as he climbed back up and settled between Callie's thighs.

Her eyes were bright gold as she stared up at him, her lips pink and swollen, her cheeks flushed.

"Stop me if it's too much. I promise I'll never hurt you."

She reached between them, gripped him, and guided him to her core. The second his flared head touched her warmth, he shivered. He'd never experienced anything like this and he wasn't even inside of her yet.

Even though it tortured him, he slowly eased into her, watching her face for any indication she was in pain. Her hands were on his forearms as held his weight off her, his elbows locked. His muscles ached with the need to thrust into her.

"Are you okay?" he asked when he'd pushed almost fully into her. She nodded, but he could tell she was holding her breath. "Breathe, Callie." She released her breath and giggled, bringing a smile to his face.

When their pelvises were touching and he was fully inside of her, he waited while her body adjusted to him, stretched around him. "Please," she begged, gripping his ass and urging him on. "Please move."

He pulled back and slowly pushed back into her, circling his hips to add pressure to her swollen clit. Her eyes rolled back and her lips parted on a sigh. Holy fuck, he was dying. Micah gritted his teeth and repeated the same slow, gentle motions over and over until she pushed her hips up to meet him. And all fucking control snapped.

"Fuuuck," he growled out, dropping onto his elbows to bury his face in the crook of her neck. His hips pumped faster, and he grunted every time she met his thrusts. If she was hurting, he couldn't tell. In fact, she seemed close to falling apart.

Taking her mouth, he swiped his tongue past her lips and pushed into her harder, faster until his balls tightened.

Oh shit.

In his stupor, he'd forgotten any form of protection. As Callie cried out with her release, her body gripped him, milked him of his release. With zero thought, he opened his mouth and latched onto the flesh at the base of her throat and shoulder the same time he pulled from her and trapped himself between their bodies, grunting with each spurt of his release.

Their breaths rasped in the silence of her little place and Micah had a second where he truly felt at home. Not necessarily inside these four walls, but holding Callie, being with her, being inside of her, feeling her heart thump against his chest. It was sappy and enraging and insanity inducing, but it was the most calming sensation he'd ever experienced in his pathetic ass life.

"Callie?" he grunted out as he struggled to slow his breathing and heart rate.

"Yeah," she whispered, threading her fingers through his hair and lightly grazing her nails against his scalp.

"Are you okay?" he asked, still overly concerned for her.

She chuckled softly, the sound vibrating through her chest. "Not really. At first, it kind of stung a little, but I don't think I've ever felt that good in my life. I've officially had my first orgasm."

He lifted his head and looked down at her in confusion. "You never gave yourself one?" She shook her head. "That was literally your first orgasm ever?" She nodded and smiled up at him. Yeah; he seriously wanted to run outside and howl into the night sky. His pride pumped up until he was ready to burst. "Sorry I came on your stomach."

"We didn't use a condom," she said with a shrug. "I want to see where this goes, and I'm glad you marked me, but I don't think cubs are a good idea right now."

Fuck. He *had* marked her. Lifting onto his hands and shoving her hair away, he stared in horror at the blood seeping from her torn skin. "Shit, Callie. I'm so fucking sorry." He rushed into the bathroom, wet a washcloth, and grabbed a towel. He held the towel to her mark and cleaned her stomach off with the cloth. "I...fuck, I'm sorry."

Her brows furrowed. "Do you regret it?" Great. Now he'd hurt her feelings.

"That's not what I meant. I didn't want to hurt you."

"You didn't. I mean, it kind of pinched a little when your teeth broke my skin, but that orgasm made me forget all about it."

Orgasm and broken skin. Those two words bounced around in his head, making his wolf stir and growl. He was just as confused as to how to feel as Micah was. Pride and anger. Pride and sorrow. Pride and fear.

"You were supposed to bite the back of my neck, though." She pulled the towel away and touched her fingers gently to the ruined flesh and brought them back to examine them. "Not even bleeding anymore."

"I couldn't take you from behind and not fuck you senseless." Maybe her kind didn't need to fuck to bond, but with how things were going, if he'd turned her to bite the back of her neck, he would've ended up bending her over and slamming deep into her.

"That doesn't exactly sound bad," she purred. Literally purred. And her eyes were bright gold again.

"Your first time is not the time for that. Next time."

But he honestly didn't know if there'd be a next time. She wanted him to take her from behind so he could latch onto her neck and mark

38

her. Again. She wanted him to draw blood from her. Again. He didn't know if he could do that and not lose his fucking mind even further.

∞ ∞ ∞

Holy hell. She'd officially had sex. And she was kind of, sort of mated. He'd marked her in the way the wolves did, but surely that wouldn't matter. Part of her was relieved that the lions could no longer try to claim her. But the bigger part was over the moon that she'd been claimed by her real mate, the man who was looking down at her like he wanted to kill someone.

"Will you stop, Micah?" she said, pushing his hand away as he once again inspected his mark on her shoulder.

Okay, yeah, it had ached a little, all of it. When he'd pushed his thick finger into her, she'd felt something pinch and then the pain was gone. She'd had her first orgasm and it was by Micah's amazing mouth. It was a tad more painful when he'd finally slid his long shaft into her, but she'd stretched to fit him. She needed him to move and eventually had to take the reins. Even after begging, he'd taken it so slow with her, had been so gentle.

Who'd have thought the pissed off guy from the first night would be so sweet and caring? So attentive. She could tell the whole time they made love he was barely hanging on by a thread, so she'd pushed her hips up to meet his, urging him on, making his dick slide in deeper, harder.

She'd really just wanted to make him feel as good as he'd made her. So, when the second orgasm bloomed low in her belly, it had caught her by surprise. The lionesses in her old Pride had told her females didn't orgasm through intercourse, and she'd be lucky if she ever got off while with a male. They'd encouraged her to learn how to pleasure herself, but she knew when—and she'd always believed it was *when* and not *if*—she found her real mate, he'd know how to take care of her, how to make her feel like a sex goddess.

And oh, how Micah had done just that.

"Do you regret it?" she asked for the second time.

He was relaxing a little as her Shifter healing kicked in and the bleeding had stopped. Within a day, her mark would be nothing but a scar, a reminder every day that Micah had chosen her even though they were so different.

"I told you, not at all. I just never wanted to hurt you."

"Yeah, you keep saying that," she said, narrowing her eyes at him. His whole Pack had reacted when they'd discussed the way Tammen treated their lionesses. But Micah took it to a whole other level. "Micah...did something happen? I mean, did something happen to a female you loved?" Her heart ached the second he turned empty eyes on her. Was he shutting down? Shutting her out?

"I shouldn't have marked you. It's just going to cause you more problems." He stood and pulled his jeans back on, then pulled her shorts up her legs and straightened her tank top.

Callie sat up and gawked as Micah made his way to her door. "Are you fucking serious?" she said a little too loudly. If any of his Pack were awake, they'd have heard her outburst. Then again, they would've heard what Micah and Callie had just done, too.

Micah hesitated at the door, his hand on the knob, his back to her. "I'm sorry," he said, his voice soft, his head hanging low.

He pulled the door open, stepped into the night, and pulled it closed behind him silently. He didn't look at her through the door, didn't say anything else.

And she was left wondering if she'd just been used by someone she'd thought she could trust. Had she been fooled into sleeping with him? Had the whole thing been an act so he could enact revenge on her Pride?

Pushing to a sitting position, she curled into herself and let the tears fall as her chest ached at the loss. But she wasn't sure if it was the loss of the last pure thing about her or the loss of who she thought was her mate.

All she knew was her heart was breaking and pieces of it had walked out the door with Micah.

Chapter Four

Callie had barely slept at all. Her eyes felt like they were full of grit as she scrubbed them with the heels of both hands. Stretching, she winced at the soreness between her legs, and anger and sorrow from last night crashed into her.

But she refused to shed one more tear. Not happening. That bastard had played her for a fool and she refused to allow any more weakness over another male, regardless of how hard her heart ached for him.

Voices were moving around outside her house, and she sat up and made her way to the front door. Everyone was piling into their trucks to head off to work and start their days. Nova walked Gray to his door and kissed him before he climbed into the cab.

Reed said something to Emory that made her slap his arm and then she hugged Tristan around the waist. She waved as the first truck pulled out of their spot and walked to stand next to Nova. Micah stepped off his porch and stopped, turning his head in her direction. She backed up so he wouldn't see her watching him through the glass and waited as he shook his head and stomped to his truck. He slammed his door shut hard enough to make the truck rock, turned the engine over, then actually peeled out, leaving a cloud of smoke wafting toward Nova and Emory.

"Asshole!" Emory called out, waving the dust away from Nova's face. "What the hell is his problem this morning?" she asked. Then as if they were in sync, both women turned slowly toward Callie's house.

"Oh shit," Nova said, and then they both hurried to her porch and pushed through the front door without knocking. "Hey, hi, good morning," she said as Emory closed the door. "Get dressed."

Emory's eyes were wide as she glanced at Nova then back at Callie. Guess they knew. Then again...

Callie's hand flew up and covered the mark Micah had left on her last night.

"Too late, kitty cat. We already saw it. Get dressed. We're going out for breakfast," Nova said.

"Won't Gray be mad?" she asked as she rummaged through her new clothes.

"We're going to Moe's. I'll call him later."

"You better text him now and let him know so we won't hear about it when he gets home," Emory said, pulling her phone out and tapping out a message.

"Are you already texting him?" Nova asked with furrowed brows.

"No. I'm texting Noah to let him know we're hungry."

"Who's Moe? And who's Noah?" Callie asked, her anxiety rising. She'd only been away from Tammen for less than a week and now they were not only going into public but were apparently meeting two more men. She already had enough guy problems in her life.

"Moe's is a bar, and Noah owns it. He's with the Blackwater Clan. He's cool. And we'll be safe there, even without the big, bad Big River Pack guys with us," Nova said as she texted her mate.

Micah hadn't even given Callie his number. She couldn't text him if she wanted to. Anger burned her stomach as she yanked a shirt over her head that she knew would cover her mark. It didn't matter, though. Any Shifter within a certain distance would smell Micah on her.

Once Callie was dressed, had properly groomed—although she desperately wanted a long, hot shower to get Micah's scent off her—and had her shoes on, the women all piled into Nova's Audi and headed into House Springs. She pulled her little car up to a long, white building and Callie just stared through the windshield. There were three cars lined up along the front; what if someone from Tammen was inside?

"I can't go in there," Callie said, feeling a panic attack coming on.

"I already checked, Callie. It's just Noah and two guys from the Blackwater Clan," Emory said.

Another group of males. But they'd all reassured her this one wasn't like her Pride or even her family's Pride. They didn't treat women like trash, didn't force them into relationships they didn't want. She had to slow her breathing and calm down or she'd end up making a fool of herself.

Kind of like she'd done last night.

"You good, kitty cat?" Nova asked before pushing her door open. She was watching her in the rearview mirror, her eyes narrowed as if she were trying to see into Callie's brain.

Callie had always hated nicknames, but it didn't bother her when Nova did it. Instead of mocking her or ridiculing her, it seemed like Nova was using it more as a term of endearment, just as Micah had last night.

She climbed from the car and followed Emory and Nova inside, freezing in the doorway when three sets of eyes landed on her. They widened and the men all lifted their heads a fraction, their nostrils flaring as they scented the air.

The guy behind the bar grinned wide as he pulled menus from a pile behind him. "I never would've guessed in a million fucking years Micah would be the next to mate. I was sure it would be you," he nodded at Emory, "or Reed's crazy ass."

"I don't think we're–"

Nova elbowed her discreetly. "We were all pretty shocked, too," she said, but Noah narrowed his eyes at her gesture. If he suspected anything, he didn't say a word. "What's on special?" she asked as she opened the menu.

"How many times have I told you, we don't have specials. What you see is what you get," he said with a shake of his head, but his expression was soft. "How much longer?" he asked as he glanced down at her round belly.

She rubbed it as she read the menu. "At least another month or two. Hey," she said suddenly, raising her eyes to his. "What's your guess? Girl or boy?"

The bartender looked from Nova to Emory and back again. "I have no idea."

"Reed keeps saying it's a boy, but I think little Wolfgang is going to be a Wolfgang-ette."

Callie couldn't help herself; she barked out a laugh. Seriously, where did Nova come up with half of what she said? It was like her mouth just spewed the words before her brain had a chance to process what she was thinking.

"I'm sure you'll both be happy with either. I'm Noah," he said, reaching his hand across the bar. Callie slipped hers into his and squeezed lightly before jerking it back. "What can I get you ladies?"

Nova and Emory rattled off their order, but Callie hadn't really looked at the menu. "I'll have what they're having," she said. She could feel one of the men creeping up behind her, and her heart was racing painfully in her chest.

"Which one? They ordered two different things," he said, his eyes raising over her head.

She couldn't take it. Whipping around on her stool, she prepared to Shift so she could protect herself, or maybe even Emory and Nova.

But the man behind her wasn't even looking in Callie's direction. He was reaching his arms out to Nova. "Hey, lady. Got your text. Take it this is the new girl," he said as he hugged Nova around the shoulders then jerked his head toward Callie.

"Yep. This little kitty is officially part of the Big River Pack. And you know, as my new best friend, it's kind of your job to protect her." Nova winked at Callie. "Callie, this is Colton from Blackwater. Colton, this is Callie Kitty."

Callie frowned at Nova but a smile stretched her lips. Every time Nova opened her mouth, she amused Callie in one way or another.

"Well, nice to meet you, Callie Kitty." His eyes dipped to her covered mark. Even though he couldn't see it, he knew. He held a black cowboy hat in his hands, turning it over and over as he shook his head slowly. "Shame you met Micah first. You really are pretty," he said. "Of course, not as pretty as my best friend, here," he said, and smiled at Nova.

"You're such a flirt. I'm telling Gray," Emory said, and swatted him away when he tried to hug her. "Ew. Go." Her words were said with a giggle.

Colton stepped back, chuckling. "You need anything, you call. We'll be there. Nice to meet you, Callie Kitty," he said again, nodding and stepping back to join his other massively large friend at the table.

"Holy crap, he's big," Callie blurted out, causing the other two women to laugh.

"They're all big," Emory said, pointing at Noah. "There's one more you haven't met, the Alpha, but I'm sure you'll meet him eventually."

Okay. These guys weren't scary. She was safe. She was still pissed and hurt about last night, but she couldn't think about that right now. There was nothing she could do, so she finally focused on the menu and ordered food.

Turning on her stool to face her new friends, she looked around the room. "A Shifter bar?" she asked. She had no idea things like that existed. This must be where the guys from Tammen went all the time when Brent would come to her reeking of alcohol.

"Technically. But humans do wander in sometimes. Just make sure there are none in here before you go all feral cat," Nova said. "Noah, we need some girl time. Could you bring the food to us when it comes out?"

"Of course."

Nova and Emory led Callie to the back of the room, then they dipped their heads close to her. "What happened?" Nova asked immediately.

"I don't know if I–"

"Talk," Emory said with a sharp nod of her head.

She looked from face to face and they wore matching angry expressions. But she could tell they were angry *for* her, not *at* her.

Callie opened her mouth and let everything spill out. By the time she'd finished, tears were welling in her eyes and spilling over her lashes. "Did he just use me to get back at Tammen? Was I a revenge screw?"

"Noooo," Nova said, shaking her head.

"Micah can be jerkish, but he's not cruel. What happened before he took off? Like, did he come inside of you and freak about kids or something?" Emory asked, exchanging a look with Nova.

"That happened to me and Gray," Nova explained.

"No. It was nothing like that. He kept getting all weird about all the blood. He kept saying he hurt me and I tried to explain to him that the bite didn't hurt that—"

"He freaked about the blood?" Emory said, narrowing her eyes.

"Yeah. That's not the point," she said, waving her hand dismissively. "He kept getting really weird about it, almost like he was comparing what we'd done, the tiny, itty bitty amount of pain he'd caused me, to what the Tammen Pride did. I asked him if someone he'd loved had been hurt. And he just kind of...shut down. He got dressed and bam, he was out of there."

Emory and Nova leaned back and seemed to have some kind of secret conversation with just their eyes. It was Nova who spoke first. "Do you know anything?"

"Not a damn thing. I don't even know if Gray knows Micah's past," Emory said.

"None of you know why he acts like that?" Callie asked, looking back and forth between them.

They shook their heads. Had she hit some raw nerve? Or had she been right about being revenge for some wrong done to him by someone from Tammen or another group?

"Did you mark him?" Nova asked.

Callie shook her head. "No. Lionesses don't mark their males. Only the females get marked."

"But Micah's a wolf. Not a lion," Emory said.

He hadn't asked her to bite him. Hell, he hadn't asked much more than whether she was sure and if he'd hurt her. "He only marked my shoulder, though. That's not how lions mark."

"And again, he's a wolf. He marked you as his mate, Callie. So, whatever happened last night? It's not over. Not by a long shot. I'd talk to him when he gets home from work. Tell him he was being an asshat. Make him apologize," Nova said.

"Or you can do like Nova. Get drunk and pick a fight with someone from another group," Emory said, pressing her lips into a thin line to hide the smile.

"Hey, that wasn't on purpose. Those guys just irked me," Nova said, leaning back and rubbing her belly again. She winced lightly.

"You okay?" Callie asked. She'd seen so many women carry cubs. It never seemed very pleasant.

"Yeah, I'm good. She keeps kicking my bladder, though." The look on Nova's face was nothing short of loving. This was what motherhood was supposed to look like. This was what family was supposed to look like.

As the conversation turned to possible name choices and whether or not Gray and Nova would try for more, the door opened and Emory stiffened as her eyes widened. "Oh shit," she breathed out.

The world moved in slow motion as Callie straightened her spine and turned. Brent. And Eli. Eli wouldn't hurt her, at least she hoped not, but Brent looked murderous. His nostrils flared, his eyes blazed the brightest gold she'd ever seen, and his hands were balled in fists as he stalked to where the three women sat tucked into a corner at the back of the bar.

Callie stood so fast she knocked her chair over and searched for an exit close enough to reach before Brent got to her. She watched in terror as his eyes swept over her body and zeroed in on where Micah had marked her last night. How did he know? Even if he smelled the wolf all over her, how did he know where Micah had bitten her?

"Brent!" a booming voice called out.

Brent and Eli stopped and turned their head toward Noah, a sneer bringing up the corner of Brent's lip. "She's mine," he snarled.

"Not happening, brother," Noah said, stepping around from the back of the bar.

"I'm not your fucking brother."

Colton and the other big guy he was sitting with slowly rose and moved to block Brent's path to Callie, Nova, and Emory. They stood with their arms crossed over their barrel chests and glared at Brent.

Emory yanked her phone from her back pocket and hurried out a text. "They're coming," she whispered, but Brent heard her.

His eyes narrowed on Emory's phone clutched in her hands. "Yeah. You should definitely tell them to come here. I think Micah and I need to have a little talk about messing with someone's mate."

Oh, that was definitely a threat. He'd beaten her physically, tried to break her mentally, and now he stood there trying to lay claim on someone who wanted nothing to do with him. "I'm not your fucking mate, Brent. I never was and I never will be. I have a mate. And he's a hundred times the man you can ever hope to be." She yanked her shirt to the side and showed off the mark, lifting her chin and keeping eye contact, refusing to look away even when her knees shook and threatened to give out from under her.

"He broke the fucking law," Brent said, his voice no longer resembling a man, just beast.

"Fuck you. I never belonged to you. I don't belong to anyone." Callie put her shirt back in place and crossed her arms. She didn't look nearly as intimidating as the bears from Blackwater, but she just hoped it got her point across.

Brent, being the idiot he was, moved toward her again. But Colton and his friend just took equal steps in his direction, their arms no longer crossed, their hands ready to grab him and throw him out on his ass.

"Come on, man. I just want to eat," Eli said, slapping a hand on Brent's shoulder and attempting to pull him back.

"Not in here. Get him the fuck out of my bar," Noah said, joining his Clan brothers to block Brent's path. Hell, their large bodies were partially blocking the view to Callie. She looked behind her to make sure there were no doors or windows for anyone to sneak up on her, and sighed with relief when she realized, once again, she was safe from Brent's anger.

"Fuck you, Noah. I can get this place closed down in an hour," Brent said, turning his ire on the big bear Shifter. Three humongous guys versus two lion Shifters. Hell, Callie and Emory would probably join the fight just to make sure Nova was safe. Three bear Shifters, a lioness, and a wolf? Brent would be fucked.

"Can he do that?" Callie asked, her eyes moving to Noah's back. He turned his head a little but didn't pull his eyes from Brent.

"Fuck no. This was my dad's place. He has no say over what the Blackwater Clan does," Noah said with a smirk.

Brent jammed a finger in Noah's direction. "We'll see, fucker. Callie," he called out, moving his eyes and his finger to her now. "Get your ass home. Now. Or risk your little friends."

Callie looked over at Emory and Nova, true fear for their safety burning her gut. She took a step forward. The last thing she wanted to do was go with him, to be subjected to constant beatings when she had to fight him off her body, but she wouldn't endanger the people who'd taken her in and made her feel like she belonged.

The front door opened and three bodies blocked the sun pouring in. Even with their faces shadowed, she knew who was there. Her mate. He'd come. When he stepped further into the room, Callie actually felt a little bad for Brent. Micah's eyes were almost glowing they were so bright blue and his teeth had partially Shifted. Holy shit. She'd never seen someone so out of control of their animal before.

"Get the fuck away from my mate," Micah growled. No. Not Micah. His wolf. He lithely moved across the room and stood a foot from Brent. Gray put a hand on his shoulder while Reed moved to stand to the side of both of them, ready to step in the middle if needed.

"You can't mate with a claimed female, asshole," Brent said, jabbing Micah in the chest with his index finger.

Micah swung his arm, knocking Brent's finger away and reached for him, aiming straight for his throat.

"Stop! Micah, stop," Callie pleaded, pushing through the wall of bodies guarding her. "Please. He's not worth a fight. We'll just go."

"You coming home?" Brent said, never pulling his eyes from Micah.

"Not with you, asshole," she said, stepping behind Micah. She knew better than to get between two dominant Shifters, especially when they were fighting over her. It would just send Micah crazy having Brent so close to her. "I'm going home with my mate." She still had no idea what had happened last night, why Micah had run away the way he did, but he'd taken her innocence and claimed her with his mark. Whether he wanted her forever or not, she was physically bound to him now.

"I'm your fucking mate, whore!" Brent roared and lunged for her.

Callie brought her hands up to block him, but Colton locked an arm around his throat and dragged him back the same time Gray, Reed, and Noah shoved at Micah, pushing him away before he killed Brent and truly caused a war between the groups.

"Get him the fuck out of here before I let Micah rip his throat out," Noah said breathlessly as the three Shifters fought to keep Micah back.

He was snapping his fangs, growling and snarling, the tips of his fingers Shifted into claws as he tried to drag himself to Brent.

Colton half carried Brent to the door and kicked it open. Eli shook his head slowly, a sad look in his eyes as he followed Brent. He knew something the rest of the guys didn't, something Callie was fully aware of. This was far from over. Brent wouldn't stop until he impregnated Callie, regardless of whether she was mated to Micah. Or he'd kill her. He followed Colton and Brent outside and pushed the door closed, shutting the rest of them in and cutting off the protests from Brent.

"Should someone go help Colton?" Callie asked as panic caused her body to tremble.

Nova snorted from a few feet behind Callie. "Colton picked me up like I was a feather. That butthole is stronger than anyone I've ever met. I kind of hope Brent picks a fight with him. He deserves to get his ass kicked by the big bear."

Callie turned. "Why the hell are you so close? You could've gotten hurt." Callie reached both hands for Nova's belly, then yanked them back. "Are you okay? Is Wolfgang okay?" she asked.

Nova waved her off. "Oh, please. Our guys fight all the time. Just give it time and you'll get used to it, too."

Emory didn't look like she was used to it. Her eyes were wide, her breath came in pants, and her focus was glued to the closed door. Callie turned to her, ready to comfort her, to put her mind at ease, but hands roughly grabbed her and whirled her around.

She yelped, for a second unsure of who was touching her, but gasped when Micah's mouth crashed over hers. And then she was lost. She was lost in his touch, in his mouth, lost in his taste, his scent, his passion.

His tongue swiped into her mouth and he kissed her desperately, one hand tangling in her hair and tilting her head back, the other crushing her against his trembling body. She wasn't sure if it was from his kiss, from relief, or from the dominance rolling from him, pulsing off him and crashing into her, but she experienced a power she'd never felt but relished. For a second, she felt stronger, ready to take on anyone and anything, as long as Micah kept holding her like that.

"We need to talk," Noah said, breaking the spell Micah had put her under.

With a long, low growl, Micah ended the kiss, leaving a few soft pecks to her lips before pulling away from her completely. She was left gulping air into her lungs and swaying on her feet. What the hell had he done to her? She felt like she'd drank a bottle of whiskey.

Micah's eyes darted to her a few times, but he followed Colton, Noah, and the other guy to a table. Gray immediately made his way to Nova, brushing his hands over her hair, and dipped to press a kiss to her round belly. Reed had an uncharacteristic scowl on his face as he stood with Emory, dipping his head to line up his sight with hers.

"You good?" he asked, narrowing his eyes on hers.

"Yeah," she breathed out, peeling her eyes from the door and looking up at Reed. "Yeah. I'm fine. Are you okay?" she asked Callie.

Callie stood staring as if in a trance. She nodded, but her head felt like it was no longer attached to her shoulders. Reed wrapped an arm around both women and led them to the table filled with big, dominant Shifters. Micah growled at Reed's embrace, but didn't say anything.

Nova sat between Gray and Noah, Emory sat between Reed and Callie, and Callie sat directly beside Micah. He grabbed her chair and pulled it closer until their thighs were touching under the table.

"What the fuck just happened?" Gray asked, one arm around Nova, the other laying on the table.

"They let me know they were coming for breakfast, so I called Luke and Colton in, just in case," Noah said as he leaned back in his chair, his legs splayed in front of him. He was the only one not leaning on the table. His eyes kept going to the door, waiting for Colton to return. When the big cowboy came back, a grin on his face, Noah relaxed a little more.

"You couldn't wait for one of us?" Gray asked with a frown.

"Wolfgang needed food. Besides, we were fine. Did it look like we weren't fine?" she asked, her brows raised in innocence.

"We wouldn't have let those dickheads touch them," Colton said, grabbing a chair, flipping it around, and straddling it. Callie had no idea how any of the bears even fit on the chairs.

"You had plenty of food at the house," Gray said, still focusing on Nova.

"Yeah, but we needed girl time. And in case you haven't noticed, our sheds aren't exactly big. And I'm even bigger than before," she said, once again stroking her belly, making circles around it with the palm of her hand.

Callie's heart warmed at the sight of the sweet couple beside her, but she started when a hand landed on her thigh beneath the table. She looked up at Micah, but he wasn't looking at her; his attention was on the conversation going on around them. His claws and fangs had retracted, but his eyes were still bright. They didn't have that stunning glow anymore, but they hadn't bled back to his normal blue-green.

"No more wandering into town without us," Micah said, finally tilting his head down to look Callie in the eye.

"Come on," Nova whined. "We were totally fine."

"That mother fucker could've taken her, Nova," Micah said, raising his voice.

"Careful," Gray said, a soft growl lacing his words.

Micah closed his eyes and took a few deep breaths. When he opened them, his eyes were normal, but Callie could still feel the tension wafting from him.

"Were you going to go with him?" Luke asked, snapping her out of the same fog she sank into every time she looked into Micah's eyes.

"What?" she asked, shaking her head to shake the haze away.

"You looked like you were going to just walk out of here with him," Luke said, leaning forward and resting both forearms on the table.

"He threatened to hurt them," she said, nodding to the people around her. Her stomach turned at the thought of anything happening to Emory or Nova.

"It was an empty threat," Reed said, pushing back from the table and folding his arms over his stomach.

"I don't think so," Emory spoke up. Her eyes were unfocused as she stared across the room. "That other guy with him? Eli? He actually looked nervous, and I've never seen any of those guys nervous about anything."

"Of course, he looked nervous. They were outnumbered," Colton said with wide grin.

"I think it was more than that. I think he's worried about what Brent was going to do...or is going to do."

"Brent said we broke a law," Callie said, turning to Micah.

"No. He said *he* broke a law," Nova corrected her, lifting her chin and gesturing toward Micah.

"Is that true?" Callie asked.

"Fuck him," Micah said, turning and giving Callie his profile. His jaw was clenched so tight a muscle ticked in his cheek.

"Is it? Did we break a law by what we did last night?"

"Yeah. About that. What the fuck happened last night?" Gray asked.

Heat rushed Callie's chest, moved up her neck, and settled in her cheeks. She seriously did not want to go into details with all these people. The thought of telling them she'd finally lost her virginity at twenty-two years old to a man she'd barely just met and knew as her mate was too much to reveal.

"I marked her," Micah said, lifting his chin as if to challenge any protests.

"Is she your mate?" Gray asked.

Micah looked back down at Callie, and as it always did, the world seemed to fade away. She was still pissed. She was still hurt. But her lion was purring in her head and Callie's heart swelled with affection. He was hers. Technically, she was his. Lionesses didn't claim males, they didn't mark them, they were obedient and bred for the species, did their duty to increase their numbers.

But last night, Micah had made her feel like she was so much more, like she was worth so much more.

"Yes," Micah said without looking away from her. He kept his gaze locked on hers, his eyes dipping to her lips before raising back to her eyes.

Callie couldn't hold back the smile that one word did to her heart if she had to save her own life.

"Fuck," Gray muttered.

"Fuck is right," Reed agreed with a slow shake of his head. "Tammen ain't going to let this go, Micah."

Staring at her for a few more heartbeats, Micah reached up and cupped her cheek before dropping his hand and turning to Reed. "Fuck Tammen. Fuck Brent. Fuck them all."

"I swear I just had a case of déjà vu," Nova said, smiling. Emory wasn't, but she squared her shoulders as if ready for whatever was coming their way.

As Callie looked around the table, she realized they had the same expression on their faces; they were resolved to the idea of a fight. These people were willing to put themselves between her and whatever Brent laid at her feet. She hated the thought of anyone getting injured because of her, but she hated more the thought of being away from Micah. Just the short time since he'd left her side last night had been torture. When she didn't know whether he'd ever touch her again, whether she'd ever feel his arms around her again, she'd felt her heart splintering as pieces stretched, reaching for its other half.

"Well," Gray said, dragging a hand down his face roughly. "I guess I'll be the first to say welcome to Big River Pack."

"Would that make us a Pack-Pride now? Or a Prack?" Nova said with a confused frown between her brows.

Reed snorted and shook his head. "We've got to get back to work."

"I'll get them home and meet you guys at the site," Micah said, turning to look down at Callie again. This time, there was a different emotion in those eyes she could get lost in. Hunger. Anger. Heat. Affection...fear.

She had no idea what kind of threat, what kind of future was stretched out before them, but she knew she had allies. She finally had people who cared about her and her happiness. And they'd never give her up.

Chapter Five

Micah had freaked out. He didn't want to talk about his past. He'd thought he might be able to finally confide in someone like Callie, but the second she'd asked whether someone he'd loved had ever been hurt by someone like the Tammen fucks, he'd shut down.

And had wounded Callie.

He'd seen the way her face fell when he'd jumped to his feet and gotten dressed last night. He'd heard her pained sound when he'd stepped through her door. But he'd done it to protect her. What the fuck had he been thinking? She was a claimed lioness, yet he'd marked her, claimed her as his mate. Those assholes lived by different rules. Technically, Callie was already off limits, even though she'd never let anyone inside of her nor leave their mark.

By the Pride laws, he'd fucked up.

And now, there was no way to take it back.

But did he really want to? Did he want to sever all ties from that incredible woman? Could he stay away from her, keep his eyes and hands off her after hearing her moan his name when she'd experienced her first orgasm?

Holy fuck. He'd taken her virginity. He'd never done that; never been with someone who had zero experience in the bedroom. And he'd never been so fucking gentle.

Of course, seeing the blood from her sex and the torn flesh from his bite made him go a little nuts. And then he'd screwed up further by abandoning her when he should've been holding her, comforting her, letting her know that what they'd done was unavoidable. Hell, even if he'd waited another year, ten years, he still would've ended up claiming her.

And then, like the fucking nut job he was, he'd avoided all contact with her the next morning and headed into work like nothing had happened. He'd seen her watching him through the glass in her door. Had seen her back up in hopes of staying hidden. And he'd seen the pain etched deep in the lines of her face, seen the lavender crescents under her eyes from lack of sleep.

He knew the feeling. He hadn't slept at all since he'd left her place. He'd just stayed up all night, staring at the ceiling and arguing with his wolf. His animal was clawing at his brain, trying to force him to go back to Callie. Callie quieted his animal, settled him in a way nothing else did.

Micah had tried to protect her. Had tried to protect her from both the Tammen Pride and himself. And all he'd done was tie her permanently to his crazy ass.

Trying to distract himself as much as possible, at least until he was able to get back into their territory and try to smooth things over with Callie, he threw himself into work, ignoring the jabs from the others as they worked on a row of new houses.

"Micah!" Gray barked out as he jogged over. "We've got to go, man." The fear and anger in his eyes was all it took. Something was wrong. Something to do with the females of their group. Something to do with Callie.

His knee had bounced the short drive from the work site to Moe's, where Nova's car was parked along the front. As soon as he'd stepped out of the truck, the scent of Tammen hit him full force and he all but ripped the door from its hinges to get inside, to get to Callie.

That fucker Brent had come for Callie. And she actually looked like she was taking a step toward Brent, but it didn't exactly look like she was doing it out of her own free will.

The rest of the events unfolded as if he were watching it through a periscope. His vision had tunneled and his wolf had pushed him back, taking over Micah's body without fully Shifting. Even if Micah hadn't known the blonde stunner was his, his wolf had no problem forcing the bond. But it had been Micah who'd made the move, it had been his human side who'd wanted Callie, wanted her as his own, wanted to bury himself deep in her and make her forget about any man in her past or future.

Before Micah could kill Brent for calling Callie a whore, they'd both been torn apart, although it had taken three males to keep Micah from killing the bastard where he stood. How dare that mother fucker even look at his mate, let alone taunt her with vile names.

She'd looked pale when he'd arrived, but that fire was back in her eyes. When she realized she was truly safe…no, when she realized her new friends were safe, the Alpha's pregnant mate and the smallest member of their Pack was safe, she'd stood up for herself, let Brent know in no uncertain terms he'd never have her.

Micah would do whatever the fuck it took to make sure that stayed true.

And now Micah sat surrounded by his friends and admitted out loud to the fact he'd not only found his mate, but had claimed a female who was already spoken for. The lions didn't have the same rules as the rest of them. They didn't live with the same values, didn't hold their women on a pedestal. They were fucking Neanderthals and took what they wanted. It didn't matter if the woman fought against the pairing, didn't matter if she didn't want to be mated. Once a dominant lion chose or the female's family chose for her, her fate was sealed.

Fuck that. Fuck Brent. Fuck Tammen. Fuck their laws.

He had no doubt all of this would come down to a challenge, but he also had no doubt he'd win against that asshole. And if by some miracle Brent took Micah out, he knew his Pack and friends would keep her safe and out of Brent's paws.

"He won't stop," Callie said, her voice almost a whimper.

He hated the fear in her eyes, hated anyone who had put it there, hated anyone who'd hurt her. But he'd been one of those people who'd caused her pain. And he'd make damn sure he fixed it. He didn't deserve her, he was fully aware of that, but she'd chosen him back, had allowed his mark, had allowed him to make love to her.

Micah would spend the rest of his life making it up to her, earning her affection and trust back, earning her respect.

Looking down into her beautiful golden eyes, he realized those words were for him alone. She was warning him. Was she actually afraid for Micah? "I'll protect you," he said, feeling his heart soften as he studied her face, committing every freckle across her nose to memory.

"Seriously. We've got to get back to work," Reed said again.

The entire table rose as one, and Colton and Luke followed them outside, following them back into Big River Territory until the women were safe at home. "I'll hang out for a while," Colton said, shoving his cowboy hat back off his forehead. "I'm off today, anyway."

It was Micah's job to protect Callie. He should have been the one to take care of her. But when the threat of Brent coming for revenge was over, he wanted to be able to take care of her for the rest of her life, and he couldn't do that if he was unemployed.

Gripping Callie gently by the arm, he pulled her close and wrapped his arms around her until he heard her whoosh out a breath.

"Too tight," she squeaked out. He let go immediately, but she was smiling up at him. "Will you talk to me after you get off work?"

Pushing his fingers through her hair and tucking a wayward strand behind her ear, he nodded. He wanted to take her lips again, wanted to drag her into the house and cover her in his scent. Instead, he bent and kissed her forehead, lingering there as she clutched his shirt in both hands.

"I'll see you in a couple of hours."

He looked over her shoulder at Colton, who nodded. Like Reed, Colton was rarely serious; life was one big fucking party to him. But now, he looked like a warrior, ready to defend the women in their Pack with his own life.

"I've got 'em," Colton said, crossing his arms over his chest.

∞ ∞ ∞

The men had to go back to work, but they wouldn't be left alone. Didn't seem to matter to the Alpha.

Gray kissed Nova once, hugged her shoulders, then pointed his finger at her. "Keep your butt here until I get home. Got it? I'm serious, Nova." She rolled her eyes and stuck her tongue out at him, but he just smiled and shook his head. He did that a lot. "I love you."

"Love you, too, Papa Wolf." As the men climbed into two trucks, Nova pressed her palm to her lips and blew him her love.

Micah held onto the frame of the truck and watched Callie until they turned. There were no sweet words, no hugs, no playful teases, no blown kisses. But she'd felt everything he didn't say in that look.

When the trucks were no longer in sight, Colton pulled a chair across the clearing and waited. "Where are you ladies going to hang out?"

"Are you seriously going to sit outside the shed all day?" Nova asked.

"Yep."

With a frustrated sigh, Nova nodded at the chairs. "There's not enough room to play girl party in any of our places. We'll just hang out here with you." She plopped down in a chair and looked at Emory with an evil glint in her eye. Hiding a smile, she screwed her face into a serious look and turned to Callie. "I've got to tell you, this little puppy has me peeing twenty times a day. And, even this big, I'm constantly horny. Like, I can't get enough of Gray's di—"

"Okay. Nope," Colton said, lunging to his feet, shoving his fingers into his ears, and pacing away. "I'll be close. Holler if you need me."

Callie slapped a hand over her mouth and giggled. This life, these people, her new Pack was hilarious. Every single one of them. Well, Micah was kind of intense and a little on the broody side, but she liked it. Did the women in the Prides even know what life was like outside that world? Did they know the happiness they could have if they fought for their freedom?

"Well," Emory said once Colton moved until he was barely along the tree line circling the clearing. She'd seemed to recover from the shock at the bar. "Looks like you and Micah made up."

"Oh yeah," Nova said, leaning her head back and closing her eyes. "Hey, would I look like a beached whale if I put on a bikini?" Emory and Callie both snorted. Yeah, her belly was big with a growing pup, but the woman's curves were what inspired artists through history. Callie had never hated her body, but she'd kill to have the hour glass body of the Alpha's mate.

"You'll get sunburned," Emory said with a smile. She turned back to Callie. "I wouldn't let him off too easily. Make him grovel."

"Make him cook you dinner. Dude can cook," Nova said as she shifted in her lawn chair.

Callie looked at the pile of ruined chairs from the night she'd showed up there. One of them was a long, chaise type. Nova would've been way more comfortable in it but now it was just a mangle of metal and vinyl. Guilt made her curl her nose.

"I'll get you some new chairs if I ever get a job," Callie blurted out.

Nova picked her head up and cocked an eyebrow at her. "What? Where the hell did that come from?"

Callie pointed to the ruined furniture. "I ran over your chairs. And the firepit. I'll replace them when I can get a job."

"Oh, whatever. I wanted some new stuff, anyway," Nova said, putting her head back and closing her eyes again.

Emory winked at Callie with a smile. "Just let it go. You won't win when it comes to spending money."

"Back to the juicy stuff," Nova said. "I want all the details from last night. We got rudely interrupted. What's Micah like? You already told us you banged and got marked, but I want to know everything."

Callie looked to Emory for help, but the tiny brunette shrugged. "She's a romance writer, remember? She pretends it's research, but I think she's secretly a pervert."

"I resemble that remark," Nova said without missing a beat. "Spill."

How much could she say without making a fool of herself? Or pissing Micah off. Then again, it was just as much her business as his. And she'd never had girlfriends before. It was nice to have someone to talk to, someone to just hang out with without being indoctrinated with more nonsense about her duties as a good lioness.

"He was sweet. And gentle," Callie said softly after a few moments.

"Micah was sweet?" Nova said, opening one eye without raising her head. "Micah, as in the Second of the Pack? That Micah?"

Callie chuckled softly and shook her head. "Yeah. That Micah."

"More. I need more details," she said nonchalantly, and closed her eye again.

"What do you want to know?"

"Well, for one thing, did you finish?" Nova asked.

"Finish?"

"You know. The big O. The toe curler."

"Seriously, Nova?" Emory asked, but she was laughing. And then she turned her eyes to Callie. "Actually, I'm a little curious now, too."

Crossing her legs, Callie squeezed her thighs together as memories from their night ran through her mind. Up until the moment he'd pulled the wham-bam-thank-you-ma'am act, it had been the single best moment of her life.

"He...um...he was my first."

Both women sat straight up and stared wide-eyed at her. "What?" they both whisper-screamed at the same time.

"Wait...how old are you, Callie? I mean, you're not one of those seventeen-year old girls who looks like an adult, are you?" Nova asked.

"No! I'm twenty-two." She'd told Emory how long she'd been with Tammen on their ride to the hardware store, but she must not have told Nova.

"But you said you were with Tammen for six years," Emory said, narrowing her eyes as her brows lowered.

"Right," Callie answered.

"And no one...you know," Emory said.

"No. We've already discussed this. I refused to let Brent or anyone else touch me."

"But I mean...with no one? Ever? You never even had a boyfriend or anything?" Callie shook her head. "Hold on...okay, I've got to wrap my head around this." Nova put her fingertips to both temples then her eyes flew wide. "Oh man. I totally need to write a book about this."

"Oh my gosh. Please don't do that." Shit. She should've kept her mouth shut. Nova had gotten in trouble for writing about Shifters and now she was going to put Callie in a book.

"No, no. Not really. Just...yeah, a virgin who falls for some tough on the outside, mushy on the inside country boy. That is going to be one hot book."

"Did he hurt you?" Emory asked, steering away from Nova's talk of using Callie as inspiration.

"Not really. It was more uncomfortable when he used his fingers, but he made me forget about it with his mouth," Callie said, heat burning her cheeks.

"Now we're talking," Nova said, pretending to fan herself. "More, more, more."

"You watch porn a lot, don't you?" Emory teased.

"Research," Nova muttered.

"Whatever," Emory said with an eyeroll.

"And? What about the sex?" Nova said, ignoring Emory.

"I don't know. It's not like I have anything to compare it to...but it felt really good."

"And you achieved toe curling," Nova said, rolling her head on the headrest to look at Callie.

"Twice," she admitted.

"Swoon," Nova said, putting the back of her wrist and hand to her forehead theatrically. "I never would've guessed Micah as a gentle lover. I always pictured him going buck wild, you know, like pounding into his woman and grunting all caveman like."

"There was definitely some grunting," Callie blurted out before she could catch the words.

Nova and Emory exchanged a look then busted out laughing. "I wish you could see your face right now. You're in total la-la land. I bet I know what happens tonight," she said, her voice going song like in the end.

"Guess Tristan and I need to get soundproofing, too," Emory said, fist bumping Nova.

"What?" Callie asked.

"Reed put up this foam stuff all over the wall closest to me and Gray when I got here. Said he was tired of hearing us bump uglies all the time," Nova explained.

And there was the heat in her cheeks again. No one had heard them last night because they were all asleep. But, if Micah and Callie were able to work through his demons and make this thing work, there were definitely going to be a lot of noise complaints. Because after what Micah had given her last night, she badly wanted more.

Trucks came rumbling down the drive three hours later and Nova climbed to her feet, her hand at her back as she stretched. "'Bout damn time," she grumbled. "I'm starving."

"I could've made you something," Callie said, her eyes on Micah's truck as it followed Gray's. But there were more vehicles following. They had company.

"Nah. I texted Gray and asked for some chicken nuggets. He better have gotten the twenty piece this time."

Callie was barely paying attention as she watched men she'd never met climb from their trucks. Colton had trekked across the field and was shaking hands with a few guys and fist bumped a man as big as he was. Must have been the Blackwater Alpha she hadn't met yet.

Micah didn't wait for the rest of the men, just made a beeline for Callie. She stood and closed the space, walking straight into his open arms.

"I'm sorry for last night," he said into her hair. He smelled like fur, saw dust, and sweat, and her body instantly warmed.

"I'm sorry, too."

He pulled back, his arms still wrapped around her, and frowned down at her. "No. You don't get to be sorry for anything. I was the dick. I'm the one who treated you like crap." He shook his head. "No apologies, okay. It'll just make me feel like a bigger shit."

"You are a big turd," Emory said as she passed and greeted the guys.

"Who are those guys?" she asked, looking past him.

He turned, his arm draped over her shoulder almost possessively, and started pointing at guys. He named them off, identifying them as panthers from the Ravenwood Pride and Carter, the Alpha from Blackwater Clan. No way would she remember everyone's names until she spent more time with them.

The men from the Ravenwood Pride were around the same heights as those from the Big River Pack. And they were all muscle and sinew. But where the men from her Pride were a little on the stockier, bulkier side, Ravenwood were lean, their muscles defined. The Blackwater guys were all tanks, standing close to seven feet and broad. When Carter hugged Emory, she disappeared behind his big body.

As she looked around, she realized everyone shared the same look of determination. This wasn't a social call. This was a what-do-we-do-about-Tammen meeting. And her guilt was back. It seemed that was her number one emotion in the short time she'd been with this group.

The man Micah had identified as the Alpha sauntered over to her and extended his hand but never moved in for a hug as he had with Nova and Emory. "I'm Carter, Alpha of Blackwater." She slipped her hand into his and let him squeeze it quickly before pulling back. "I hear you've got an overzealous fan."

Callie didn't know what she'd expected from Carter, maybe an Alpha more like Rhett. Where her Pride's Alpha was domineering, controlling, even cruel at times, Carter was respectful and kept his distance from the newly mated lioness. He was playful and his tone was light. His warm brown eyes crinkled at the edges as he smiled.

"Yeah, guess you can say that," she said, unable to keep from smiling back.

Colton and Luke carried over a few extra lawn chairs as everyone sat in a circle around the pile of bricks formerly known as the firepit. "What the hell happened here?" Mason from Ravenwood asked, kicking a loose brick with his toe.

"Crazy woman driver," Reed said as he carried over a large cooler and set it in the center of the circle. As everyone dove into it and pulled a beer, Nova ripped open her fast food bag and shoved a nugget into her mouth.

Micah popped the top of a beer and handed it to Callie before sitting beside her. Then he stood, pulled the chair closer to her, and sat again. She ducked her head with a smile when Emory winked at her. They'd had a rough start to their odd relationship, but Micah was letting her know he was in this with her.

"I got a call from Rhett," Carter said when everyone was settled.

Micah growled beside her and reached for her hand. He was holding on a little too tightly, but if he needed the touch to stay settled, she wasn't going to stop him.

"What the fuck did he want?" Micah asked. Callie didn't know why; everyone who knew Callie's story knew exactly why her Pride would contact another Alpha.

"Wanted to remind me that Callie was promised to Brent by her father. Told me she's already claimed and that you broke their laws. And reminded me that any interference by my Clan would be seen as a challenge."

"He's just pissed I kicked his buddy's ass," Colton said, removing his hat and setting it on his knee.

The sun was setting behind the trees and the late Spring evening was promising to be cool. Callie shrugged with an apologetic smile when Reed tried to start a fire in the middle of the brick pile and shook his head at her. But eventually he had it roaring, and the fire warmed her even though the conversation cooled her blood.

"We don't follow Pride laws. That fucker knows that," Gray said. He glanced at Micah and exchanged a look. The Alpha had his Second's back, even if it meant bringing trouble to their front door.

"That's what I told him. He called Aron, too," Carter said, tipping his beer toward the Alpha of Ravenwood.

"Told him the same thing Carter did. Told him to shove his threats up his ass sideways," Aron said.

"Yeah; that's not what I told him," Carter said with a curl of his lips at Aron's choice of words.

"Same difference."

"I'm assuming he threatened a fight?" Gray asked.

Callie's eyes bounced from one male to the other as they spoke about her as if she weren't right there. Not true. They didn't directly speak about her; they spoke about her future, about her former Pride's determination to regain one of their future breeders.

"Yep. I believe the word he used was war," Carter said. Trever had used the same word when they'd chased her onto Big River territory.

"The jackass didn't bother calling me. Pussy," Gray said before taking a long draw from his beer. "You know I'd never ask you guys to put yourselves in the middle of our shit."

"You have a pregnant female. And an unmated one. No way can we sit by and do nothing," Carter said. His Clan nodded their heads in agreement.

"I haven't had any fun in a while," Aron said.

His Pride chuckled and nodded along, as well.

"This is too much," Callie finally said, slashing her hand in the air. "You guys are talking about fighting a whole Pride over me. Me. One person. Look at her," she said, pointing at Nova, who stopped with her nugget filled hand mid-way to her mouth. "What'll happen if they come after her? She can't Shift. She can't fight. And if they get their hands on her," she said, pointing at Emory, "they won't care that she's not a lioness. They'll take her and try to breed her just to prove a point."

"The only other choice is you returning to the Pride, Callie Kitty," Nova said, recovering and shoving the nugget into her mouth. "And I'd be pretty pissed at any male sitting here who'd let that happen." She turned her glare on everyone in the circle. A few people chuckled, a few raised their hands in surrender.

"She's not going back," Micah said, his hand still tight around hers. "You're not going back. Unless you want to."

"No, of course not. I'd rather be dead." Micah's hand twitched almost painfully around hers at that statement. "But I can't live with myself if one of you are attacked because of me."

"There are more of us than them," Colton said.

"You don't understand. There are more than you realize. And the lionesses who chose to be with them will fight, too."

"I thought there were only four of them," Gray said, leaning forward and resting his elbows on his knees.

Callie snorted. "Hell no. Those are just the enforcers. Those guys get the first pick of the females. There's at least ten others I've seen come and go. They don't live within the same territory, but they're Tammen guys, through and through. It's not even an allegiance thing. Nobody really cares about anyone else in that Pride. But Rhett promises them females, power, and control."

"Fuuuuck," Reed groaned out as he flopped back against his chair. "How many lionesses?"

"There were sixteen when I was there. But only five or six of them will willingly fight. But all Rhett would have to do is threaten to remove the cubs from their lives and they'll do whatever he wants."

"So possibly nineteen or twenty lions." Reed looked around the circle, pointing and counting. "We have fourteen, fifteen if we count Callie."

"We don't," Micah said.

"You do. Fifteen," Callie said. No way would she let these people fight while she cowered when she was the cause of all of it.

"Fourteen, but four of us are bears," Colton said, crossing his ankle at his knee.

"Fifteen," Callie corrected.

"Hey, what about me?" Nova said, brushing the crumbs from her hands.

"No!" everyone said at the same time. Nova crossed her arms on top of her belly and pouted.

"But there can still be more if the other lionesses are forced to fight," Callie reminded them. She hated to think of those women who'd been broken under Rhett's rule being shoved into a fight they weren't prepared for.

"What about her? What do we do with Nova if there's a fight?" Reed asked.

"I'll take her to my dad's if those pussies actually follow through," Colton said.

"I'm still waiting to hear back from my dad. I'll ask him if there's anything the council can do to help if it comes to fisticuffs," Nova said.

Gray looked at his mate and nodded. "Not a bad idea. Colton, you talk to your dad, too. The lions' rules and laws don't apply to us, but there might be some fucked up thing that makes Brent think he still has say in what happens to Callie."

"Why don't we just kill him now?" Micah growled out.

Callie looked into his face and flinched away. His eyes had bled to his wolf's brilliant blue and his canines had elongated. How many times had he threatened to kill Brent in the short time she'd been there?

She hated all the strain she'd brought on these people, but her heart grew with the love she felt pouring from them. They didn't know her, not really, and they owed her nothing, yet they'd taken her in, given her a home and a family, and pledged to protect her no matter what.

Once again, she found herself wondering how she could ever repay any of them.

Chapter Six

Callie was half-asleep by the time everyone had climbed into their trucks and waved goodnight. Micah offered his hand and pulled her from her seat, guiding her to her house. "Will you stay with me tonight?" she asked.

Emory smiled at her as she passed and then faked a frown at Micah before climbing her stairs.

"I didn't think you'd want me to stay after last night," he admitted. He rubbed his palm over the back of his neck as if embarrassed or ashamed.

"We still have a lot to talk about, Micah. Not like we had much chance tonight." She waved her hand toward the row of taillights as they disappeared around the corner. "You promised we'd talk."

"Yeah, but you look like you're about to fall over."

She stared up into his face, nodded once, turned on her heel, and stomped to her own place. Fine. He was still playing this game. She'd thought they'd gotten somewhere after the incident at Moe's. She'd thought maybe she'd broken through the wall he'd tried to build around himself. But he'd just been placating, trying to calm her, trying to ensure she didn't leave.

She made it through her door and was pulling off her shirt for bed when a light tap on the glass made her freeze. Without turning around, she knew it was Micah. She could choose to ignore him and go to bed, but she knew sleep would evade her yet again. Or she could choose to open the door to find out what excuse he'd made this time.

Pulling her shirt back into place, she walked across the room and pulled the door open just enough to see his face. "What?" she said, and was angry at the tears burning the back of her eyes.

"I keep fucking this up," he said, his eyes sad, his lips turned down a little at the corners.

"Why did you claim me if you plan on keeping me as a part-time mate?"

"That's not what I want, Callie. I'm just scared of hurting you," he said, leaning against the door frame.

"I'm not...you know, anymore. It won't hurt."

"That's not what I meant. Wait...you still want to make love?"

"Well, yeah. Why wouldn't I?"

"Because I ran out like a fucking idiot last night," he said, dragging a hand roughly down his face. "You deserve better."

"Better than what?" She opened the door a couple inches wider.

"Better than me. Better than Brent. Hell, I don't know if there's a man alive worthy of you." He raised his eyes to her face and huffed out a breath. "Do you still want me to stay over tonight?"

She chewed on the inside of her cheek. For some reason, she'd felt safer in his house than anywhere else, but it was because he was there. Even when she'd slept inside alone, she'd known he was just a few feet away, ready to stand between her and the rest of the world.

Shoving the door, she opened it all the way and stepped back.

"You sure?" he asked, pushing from the frame. "I can sleep out here if you're scared."

"I'm not going to beg you, Micah. You either want to be with me or you don't. This back and forth stuff is what's hurting me, not anything you have in your mind."

He huffed out another of those breaths, but this one was kind of sarcastic sounding. "You have no idea."

"Well?" she said, popping out her hip and crossing her arms. "Stay or go? Which is it? Am I your mate or not?"

That got his attention. He closed the door behind him quietly, stalked forward, then stopped within inches of touching her. "You're my fucking mate. Mine. Not Brent's"

"Yours," she said.

"And I'm yours."

That caught the breath in her lungs. Lionesses didn't get to claim males. No one belonged to them, not even the cubs they carried in their bodies and birthed. But Micah was handing himself to her, handing his heart to her. He was showing her once again without even realizing it that she was free and everything she'd ever learned, all that crap they'd shoved down her throat, was nothing but a big, fat lie.

"You're mine," she whispered back.

Micah grabbed the back collar of his shirt and yanked it over his head. He stood there, watching her expectantly.

"I don't know what you're waiting for," she admitted. She was sexually inexperienced, but she knew when a man was suggesting sex. Removing his shirt and watching her wasn't exactly a green light for love making. At least not that she'd ever heard of.

"We mark our mates," he said, taking another step toward her.

"I'm not a wolf," she said as her heart raced in her chest.

"I am." His hand raised and he cupped her face. "We mark our mates. We leave a permanent scar to let everyone know our hearts are claimed."

His heart. Not just his body, but his heart, as well. He was feeling the same strong emotions she was, but neither of them would say anything out loud. Her reasoning was pure fear: fear of rejection, fear of failure, fear of losing what she'd just found.

"I told you how lions mate," she said, moving closer to him, her eyes dipping from his eyes to his firm chest.

"I'll mark you properly when I trust myself more," he said, a shy smile on his face.

"What do you mean?" she asked.

His smile widened. "You said I have to bite your neck. We truly bond while marking during sex. Do you have any idea what that's like, being fucked from behind?" For some reason, him saying *fucked* instead of *made love to* made her body go tight and sent butterflies flapping like crazy in her belly. It was so dirty. So raw and primal. Raw and primal, just like Micah.

"What if I'm ready for that now?" She looked up at Micah through her lashes, unsure of who this forward woman was, where those words had come from. And just as quickly, she realized they weren't her words, they were her animal's.

But did she agree with her lioness? Was she ready for him to take her like that?

Yes. She was.

Her words did something to Micah. His eyes flashed instantly to bright blue and his lips crashed onto hers. His hands were everywhere, on her face, her breasts, then on the backs of her legs as he lifted her and wrapped them around his waist. He carried her across the room and she gasped when she felt the rough wall hit her back. Her skin was scratched, possibly broken from the unfinished wood, but she didn't care. The sensation was nothing compared to what Micah was making her feel. She was on fire, his touch leaving goose bumps wherever his palm skimmed.

Lowering her so fast she felt dizzy, he yanked her shirt over her head, jerked one of her bra cups down and bent to take a nipple into his mouth. He licked and sucked it to a pebbled bud as his fingers worked at her jeans. Once they were to her ankles, he stepped on them so she could pull her feet out. He lifted her again, his mouth slanting over hers as his tongue invaded her mouth, dueling with hers, caressing it.

With one hand holding her under her ass, Micah reached between them and undid his pants, releasing his cock. She reached for him, wrapping her fingers around him, and guided him to her entrance. She was wet and ready for him and he slid in with ease. There was pressure, but no pain this time.

Tossing her head back, she moaned as he found a rhythm, sliding in and out of her, his breath coming fast. "Tell me if it's too much," he said, repeating what he'd told her last night.

"More," she breathed out, opening her eyes to look at him so he'd see her need.

His hips pumped harder and faster, rocking her up the wall. She felt the tiny splinters slicing through her flesh but it just spurred her on further. As the swell of an orgasm bloomed, she leaned forward, Shifted her teeth, and latched onto his chest. She broke through with ease and held on as he roared out his release, slamming into her twice before pulling from her and trapping his cock between them again, grunting with each pump of his release.

They held each other, breathing heavy, their hearts creating a matching cadence until Micah pulled her from the wall and walked her to her futon. He sat with her straddling his lap and hugged her tight to his chest. She laid her hand over his mark, trying to staunch the slow flow of blood, and listened to his breaths rasp through his chest.

Her back stung, her heart was full, and her body felt like jelly. Too many sensations, too many emotions, too much to think about. So, she didn't. Relaxing forward onto his chest, she felt the heaviness of sleep forcing her lids closed.

Micah rolled to his side and brought Callie with him. He held her as she fell asleep, kissing her temple just as she was slipping into a dream. She'd never enjoyed dreaming before, but when this one revolved around how many ways Micah would make love to her, how much time he'd spend getting to know her body, she smiled. Hopefully, as time went on, her dream would become a reality.

∞ ∞ ∞

Micah stared down at his mate with nothing short of rage. There were thin scrapes and scratches crisscrossing her pale back. He turned and looked at the wall he'd taken her against, the bare wood wall. The same wall he'd worried about her getting a splinter from. And he'd slammed her body against it and fucked her without a single thought. He was supposed to be taking care of her, supposed to be protecting her, yet he kept drawing blood from her.

He'd always known he wasn't mate material and this was just another indicator he'd been right.

Maybe it was time to stifle his pride and talk to Gray. He'd made some goofs early with Nova, but they seemed happy. He had this mate shit down. But that would mean admitting shit to Gray he didn't know if he was ready for.

He'd meant to tell Callie everything, warn her of his fucked-up animal, tell her why he was so fucking possessive over not just her but all females. Everyone thought he was a dick, he knew that, but it was easier to shut people out than to tell them he worried about getting too close for fear of losing them. He could never admit to the many nights he'd gone without sleep so he could stay outside Emory's house to make sure she was safe when Deathport was after her. Hell, they were probably still after her, but at least they'd backed the fuck off for now. One group of assholes was enough for the moment.

Shit. What if Tammen recruited Anson and his merry bunch of assholes? That would be five more against them. That would make twenty-three against fourteen, and no, he still wasn't counting Callie in the fight. He'd just convince her to stay with Nova to keep her safe. That way, he could fight without constantly worrying about her.

He was getting ahead of himself. Nova and Colton had put in calls to their dads. The council had the final say in what would happen and he had to trust the old codgers wouldn't hand an innocent woman over to the firing squad. And that's what they'd be doing. Callie would break if she were to be sent back to Tammen. And Micah would be dead because he'd challenge every single fucking lion in that Pride before he let that happen.

"Micah?" Callie's quiet voice called to him.

He turned and looked at her. Her eyes were half open, her cheeks were still flushed from their love making, and she hugged the blanket to her chest while reaching for him with the other hand. He wanted to punish himself for hurting her, but knew if he ran off again or denied her this it would hurt her worse. She hadn't reacted to any pain when they'd made love and didn't react now. And she had the same Shifter healing he did; the marks would be nothing by morning.

"What are you doing?" she asked, her voice raspy with sleep.

"Nothing. Just got a drink," he lied to her, then scooted onto the futon beside her as she held the blanket up for him. Her bed was way more comfortable than his couch. Maybe he'd spend more time with her here instead of making her cram up with him on his run-down furniture.

"You okay?" she asked as she snuggled onto his chest, pulling his arm tighter around her. He grunted his answer. "Is it always like this?" she asked, but her voice was fading as if she were falling asleep.

"Like what?" he asked, turning his head and ducking his chin so he could look at her.

"Are mates always this happy?" No more did she get the last word out than her breathing became steady and deep. She'd fallen asleep.

Were mates always this happy? He had no idea. He wasn't really even sure what he felt other than obsessed. His wolf had calmed down a little after she'd marked him, but it constantly chanted her name as if she were some goddess. Maybe she was. Because she'd managed to entrance his crazy ass.

Turning his head to nuzzle into Callie's hair, he listened to her soft breathing and stroked her arm gently. This was his mate. He'd claimed her, and now he'd pissed off her Pride to the point of threats to his entire Pack. He had to try harder. He had to fight his inner demons. He had to be honest with her.

But not tonight. Tonight, he'd enjoy her snuggled up against him and pretend he was the kind of male who deserved a woman like Callie.

****

"Wake up," Micah whispered. His lips grazed over her face, pressing onto her forehead, her cheek, then her lips. "Time to get up."

Callie groaned and rolled onto her back. "What time is it?" she grumbled. It felt like she'd just fallen asleep and now he wanted her to get up again? The sun wasn't even all the way up yet.

"It's almost seven. I have to go to work earlier since we skipped out yesterday. Nova and Emory are outside waiting for you."

Pushing onto her elbows, Callie glanced through the glass of her door. And there stood the two females of the Pack, waving with wide smiles.

"Come on, sleepy head. Time for breakfast," Nova called out.

"Ugh," Callie said, dropping back onto the futon. "I thought we were supposed to stick around here."

"You are. But you girls are going to Nova's dad's this morning. He's making breakfast and trying to figure out how to help us."

Well, that got her attention. Callie pushed all the way up and scrubbed her eyes. "But why so early?"

Micah snorted and left her side to bring her some clothes. When he returned with a sundress and some boots, she shook her head. "Jeans," she grumbled. "Is there any coffee?"

"I've got some for you," Nova called through the door, holding a travel mug up and smiling.

Emory held a matching cup in her hands and waved her out. "Come on, girl. We're hungry."

"How the hell is anyone so cheerful in the morning?" She sat up and tugged the jeans Micah handed her up her legs and over her hips. She didn't bother turning her back when she pulled on a bra and t-shirt; Shifters were naked in front of each other all the time, and Micah had already seen every inch of her body. "Give me a few minutes and I'll be out," she said to the women, shaking her head as she shuffled to the bathroom.

After relieving her bladder, she brushed her teeth and dragged a brush through her hair. Staring at herself in the mirror, she screwed up her face. She'd slept okay, but her eyes were a little puffy. She'd never been one to wear much makeup, but now she almost wished she had some concealer. Whatever. She wasn't trying to impress anyone except Micah, and he seemed to like her just the way she was.

Tying her hair back with a rubber band, she shoved the curtain out of the way and couldn't hold back the smile at Micah leaning against the countertop, wearing worn-in work jeans and a white cotton t-shirt. So yummy. And all hers.

"What time do you think you'll be home?" she asked, resting her cheek on his chest when he pulled her in for a hug. He was so much taller than she was, he rested his chin on the top of her head as he held her wrapped in his arms.

"Hopefully before dinner time. Nova wants to grill," Micah answered, pressing a kiss to her hair before setting her away from his body. "Sorry. If we stay like this much longer, I'm going to be late. Because all I want to do right now is–"

"We can hear every word you're saying, Micah. Sext her after we leave," Nova said.

Callie glanced at Nova, who'd turned her back and was leaning against Callie's door, then back up at Micah. "Sext?"

"Sexy texting. You've never done that?" he asked as he led her through her door and pulled it closed behind him.

"Uh, no. Who the hell would I sext?" She raised her brows in a *duh* manner.

"Well, now you have someone you can sext. Let's go before Wolfgang tries to eat through my pancreas," Nova said, grabbing Callie's hand and pulling her off the porch.

"Where's everyone else?" Callie asked as she tried to keep up with the hungry pregnant woman.

"Gone. Micah was supposed to ride with Reed, but he wanted to make sure you were up. I think he had other ideas before we ruined them," Emory said with a wide, shit-eating grin.

"Payback's a bitch," Micah grumbled as he followed close behind.

"Yeah. Tell you what, if I ever find a mate, or even someone who interests me enough to want to introduce to this lunacy, you have my permission to cock block as much as you want."

"Would that be pelvic blocking? Or maybe ovary obstructing," Nova said, climbing behind the wheel of her car. She wiggled side to side to fit her big belly. "Maybe you should drive. My belly's way too close to the wheel and if my seat were any further back, I couldn't reach the pedals."

Emory snorted and climbed from the passenger seat and rounded the car. Emory and Nova fist bumped in front of the hood as if they hadn't seen each other two seconds before. Such an odd friendship, but Callie loved that she was a part of all of this.

Micah leaned into the open back door and pressed his lips to Callie's. "I put my number in your phone. I'll text you later. Call me if there are any problems…or if you just miss me." He winked and stood, closing the door and backing toward his truck, his eyes on her the whole time.

"Okay; you two are kind of cute. Not as cute as Gray and me, of course, but a pretty damn close second," Nova said as Emory started the car and pulled onto the long dirt road leading them away from the Pack territory.

Turning in her seat, Callie smiled the mushiest smile she'd ever smiled as Micah stood watching her leave. He hadn't gotten in his truck, hadn't turned his back to her, just stood there and watched.

She hadn't realized she'd sighed until Emory and Nova exchanged a look and grinned. Nova turned to look at Callie over the back of her seat. "Girl, you look like a woman in love."

"Oh," Callie said, caught off guard. Love? She wasn't sure about that, but she was definitely crazy about Micah in a way she didn't understand. "I don't know about all that."

"What's there to know? Love doesn't exactly make sense. It's just...Emory, help me out here," Nova said.

"How the hell would I help? Not like I've ever been in love," Emory said, glancing at Callie in the rearview mirror and winking before turning her attention back to the road. "Nova, you've got to tell me where we're going. I've never been to your dad's."

Nova navigated, but kept looking back at Callie periodically and pressed her for more. "Does your heart race when you think about him? Like, does it do this weird pitter-patter fluttery thing in your chest?"

That was probably the best explanation of what she'd been experiencing since day one with Micah. "Yeah. A lot."

"Girl, that could just be the mate bond. You know love and mating aren't exclusive," Emory said, waving her hand in the air.

"Bull crap. Have you ever met a mated pair who didn't eventually fall in love?"

"None of the pairs in my Pride are in love," Callie said before shoving her thumb into her mouth to chew the skin around her nail.

"They're not mates or bonded. They're forced into some kind of arranged marriage thing. That's not romantic, no matter what some books say."

"You're obsessed with romance books," Emory said as she turned onto a two-lane road labeled MM.

"I'm obsessed with romance. And love. And sex. Definitely a lot of sex," Nova said, leaning her head against the rest and sighing just as Callie had.

Nova turned forward and gave Emory directions to a road off the left side of the street. They climbed an unbelievably steep driveway until a log cabin came into sight. A male who resembled Nova stepped onto the front porch, a mug in one hand as he waved the other with a wide smile on his face.

"Hey!" Nova called out as she climbed from the front seat, using the handle over her head for leverage.

"How much longer until my grandpup is here?" the man asked as he descended the stairs. He wrapped an arm around Nova and held her there, his eyes closed as he seemed to just soak her in.

"Not soon enough," Nova grumbled. "I swear I'm part elephant; it's been at least a year since Gray knocked me up."

"Ew, Nova. Don't say that to your dad," Emory complained, accepting a short side hug from the man. Callie followed close behind, just shooting him a tight-lipped smile.

"Pretty sure he knows how this happened," she said as she rubbed her stomach. "Dad, this is Callie Taylor, the kitty I was telling you about."

"Nice to meet you, Callie. I'm Alan Price."

Callie slipped her hand into his outstretched one. Every single male she'd met had offered their hand, treated her with respect, treated her like an equal. It was still a lot to get used to, but she liked it.

"You, too," she said, and returned his easy smile.

Alan led the women inside where the smell of bacon and eggs made Callie's stomach rumble. She was starving. She wasn't overly thrilled about being woken up so early, but if the food tasted half as good as it smelled, maybe it was worth the loss of a couple hours of sleep.

"Have a seat. Help yourself," Alan said as he pulled three chairs from the table and hurried to the stovetop.

There were already four plates on the table, so he just placed the plate of bacon, a plate of toast, and the skillet of scrambled eggs in the center. He moved to sit, then stood again, his butt halfway to the chair. He opened the fridge and returned to the table with butter and jelly.

Everyone ate in silence for a few minutes until Alan broke the silence. He wiped a napkin across his mouth and turned to Callie. "Nova told me you were formerly with the Tammen Pride. Who was your family Pride?"

Callie swallowed and nodded. "Yeah. I've been with Tammen for the past six years. My family Pride is Granger."

Alan sat back in his seat and whistled low between his teeth. "Granger," he repeated.

"Guess that's bad," Nova said around a mouthful of toast.

"Dude! You're getting crumbs everywhere," Emory said, covering her plate with both arms.

"Sorry," Nova said. Callie was pretty sure the crumbs that flew out of her mouth that time was on purpose.

"Yeah. It's bad," Alan said. "They've got quite a reputation."

"Reputation how?" Emory asked. She'd finished her food and pushed her plate forward. Her eyes bounced to Callie then back to Alan.

"They have no problem handing their own daughters over for the right price. They used to be set on increasing their numbers, but now I think they just depend on their lionesses popping out enough females to buy them what they want."

"That's disgusting," Nova said. She dove in for a second helping of eggs. Callie grinned at her. "What? Wolfgang's hungry. I'm eating for two now." She winked at Callie and plopped the spoonful of eggs onto her plate.

"It is. But, unfortunately, not illegal."

"Okay. So what can we do to change that?" Nova said.

"I'm not sure we can," Alan said.

"Oh, please. You're with the council. You're the law. There's got to be something."

Alan wagged his head side to side slowly, but his eyes were across the room like he was thinking. "I'll bring it up at the next meeting."

"And bring up Callie," Emory said, leaning onto her folded arms on the table top.

"What exactly is going on with you, young lady?"

"She doesn't want to be with Tammen," Nova answered for her.

"I love you, Nova, but I need to hear it from Callie." He winked at his daughter to soften his words, but she still poked her tongue out at him.

"What she said. I don't want to be with Tammen."

"Are you claimed?"

The air whooshed from Callie's lungs. How did she answer that? The only way that might actually help her; honestly. "I was given to Brent by my father when I was a teenager. I didn't want this pairing then and I don't want it now. He's cruel and he takes pleasure in hitting women."

"He hit you?"

Her heart was racing now and she wiped her palms on her jeans. With a short nod, she swallowed hard. "Yes. Many times."

"Why?"

"What do you mean why?" Emory piped in. "No man has a right to hit a woman." Alan stared at her long enough that Emory dropped her eyes. "I'm not trying to be disrespectful, but that was a messed up question."

"I'm not saying I agree with him or of anyone touching a woman. I'm just trying to get all the facts before I go to bat for her." He turned just his eyes back to Callie and waited.

"He hit me because I'd speak up for myself. He'd hit me when I told him I wasn't ready to breed, even before the time he told my father he'd wait. He'd hit me if I defended one of the other lionesses. Basically, I think he tried to find any reason he could to inflict pain on me. Or any other female who caught his eye."

"How many lionesses has he claimed?"

She hated the way he spoke of the females in her Pride. Hell, that was how all females in her species was spoken of; they were claimed. Not chosen. Not courted. Claimed. "Before I left, he had three."

"Had any of them given him cubs?"

"One. Two of them are under eighteen."

Alan's brows pulled together. "They're bringing in females that young?"

She nodded. "I was sixteen. He promised my father he'd wait until I was twenty-one, but he tried the night I came to their territory."

A low growl trickled up his throat and his eyes flashed blue so briefly she wondered if she'd imagined it.

"Just because he *claimed* her," Nova said, bending her fingers around the word, "doesn't mean anything. She's not a thing. She's a person. She's a woman. He's not her mate. Micah is."

Alan looked at Callie again. "You've found your mate?"

Nova reached over and yanked her shirt to the side, revealing her mark. "And she marked him."

"That's not where lions mark. And lionesses don't mark their males."

"Dad! She's mated to a wolf. That's how we roll. Just because they're not following someone else's rules doesn't mean squat."

"It does to her kind," Alan said, steepling his fingers under his chin. His eyes were squinted as he stared at the scar on her shoulder. "I don't know, Nova. I really don't know what we can do at this point. Technically, they both broke Pride rules."

"But Micah's not in a Pride. And she doesn't want to be."

"She's claimed, Nova. By their law, her father had every right to give up her freedom. She belongs to Tammen. She belongs to Brent."

"Bullshit, dad!" Nova said, slamming her fist on the table. "No one can just take another person's freedom! The humans call that slavery! I learned all about it when I was still in school. If *they* can outlaw that kind of crap, then surely, we can, too." Tears welled in Nova's eyes and her face was growing redder by the second.

Callie touched Nova's forearm, trying to calm her. She was way too pregnant to get so upset. But Callie couldn't speak, couldn't offer any words to console her; her own throat was closing with panic and sorrow. "I just want to be happy and free, Mr. Price," she said around the lump in her throat.

Alan studied her for what felt like an hour before nodding his head. "I'll see what I can do."

"You were able to keep me from going to jail. And you made damn sure Emory didn't fall into Deathport's hands. Just because she's not a wolf doesn't mean you can't help her," Nova said, wiping tears from her face with her soiled napkin. "I *hate* crying."

That made Callie snort but there was no laughter. Not now. Not until she knew she'd be free from Tammen or any other group who'd use her and her body for some sick power trip.

"There are lions in the council. I'll bring this to them. Try to play on their emotions. All three of them have daughters of their own."

"Did they sell them off like cows, too?" Nova said.

"Only one of them, but last I heard, she was actually happily mated to the male who'd claimed her. I'll do what I can. Okay? That's all I can promise right now. Just give me some time."

"Guess we don't have much choice, do we?" Emory said.

She was staring at Callie with so much pity in her eyes it actually stung. She wasn't just hurt for Callie, she was hurting thinking about losing her new friend. She was hurt for all the women who didn't have the lives, the choices those in the Packs did.

The conversation eventually changed over to Wolfgang and plans to build onto the back end of Gray's and Nova's house to make room for their growing family. And all Callie could think about was whether she'd be telling her new family goodbye. Micah's eyes flashed through her mind. She'd rather be dead than have to give him up. She'd rather be dead than have to tell him goodbye so she could go birth cubs for a sadistic bastard.

Chapter Seven

Micah was practically bouncing in his seat as he neared the row of houses containing his mate. He'd received only one text from Callie all day. *I miss you.* Just three words. When he'd asked her how the meeting had gone, he'd never received a reply. And her calls went directly to voicemail. Panicked, he'd called Emory; she'd told him Callie was fine, that she'd shut her phone off. And that the meeting hadn't gone as well as they would've liked.

When his truck was finally parked, he yanked the keys from the ignition, jumped from the cab, and jogged down the row until he got to Callie's. She was sitting on the porch, her knees pulled to her chin, her arms wrapped around her shins.

"Hey," he breathed out and sat on the first step. "Well?"

Her eyes rolled to his face and she shrugged. "Well, what?"

"How did it go? What did Price say?"

She sniffled once. Her eyes were puffy and red-rimmed. She'd been crying. A lot. "I'm nothing, Micah. Because I was born female, I'm nothing. I'm worth nothing more than whatever my father and another male deems enough."

"Bullshit," Micah said, his anger building with every word. "Who said that?"

"No one said that directly, Micah, but that's the way it is. It appears we did, indeed, break a law. I was already claimed. I had no right to leave, and I had no right to be mated, bonded, or marked by another male."

Micah scooted from the top step until he sat directly beside her. He slipped an arm around her shoulders and pulled her close. He pressed his lips to her temple and left them there, breathing her in. "You know I don't believe any of that, don't you?" he whispered. "None of us here do. No one believes that kind of shit except the males in the Prides. You're worth more than a life as a breeder. You deserve…I don't know, the fucking world."

She sobbed softly, but didn't say anything.

"Callie, listen to me," he said, turning her in his arms so he could look into her eyes. "I will not let that mother fucker get his hands on you. I'll run away with you, hide you in some remote cave if I have to. We'll just live like mountain men."

She snorted and a half smile appeared on her lips. "Shut up," she said, wiping away a tear that leaked over her lashes.

"I'm serious. We'll catch our food and cook it over an open fire. You can wear their hides for clothes. That'd be hot."

She slapped his chest and smiled in earnest this time. He hated how broken she seemed, how small and worthless she felt. It just made both sides of him want to kill something or, preferably, someone. Specifically, Brent.

"We can't just run away, Micah. They're not going to just let me disappear. They'll come after your Pack." She sniffled again, but straightened her legs out and squared her shoulders a little.

"It's *our* Pack, Callie. This is your Pack, too." He searched his mind for something profound to say, something that would put her at ease and comfort her; nothing. His brain was full of anger and fear.

Gray made his way slowly to Callie's porch and stood at the bottom of the stairs, his gaze locked on Micah. He dipped his head once, but Micah could see the slow burn of rage in his eyes. "Nova told me everything," he said, his voice low and full of anger. "This isn't over, Callie. You're not leaving. You're not going back to those pieces of shit." He ran a hand through his hair as a slow growl trickled from him. "What kind of fucking people just hand their daughters over to be treated like that?"

Micah knew without his Alpha saying a word he was thinking of his own child. They didn't know whether Nova would have a boy or a girl–she couldn't exactly go to the human doctors–but it didn't matter. He was going to be a father and no way could he stomach someone putting his child through what Callie's father had forced her into.

"Nova's dad said he didn't know if there was anything that could be done," Callie said, crossing her legs under her and pulling from Micah's hold. Where she'd been leaning felt cold and empty.

"I'll contact surrounding Packs if I have to. And Carter and Aron have both pledged their protection, as well."

Callie shook her head slowly, a single tear rolled down her cheek. "More lives risked. What about Nova, Gray? What about Wolfgang?"

"She'll be protected. Alan can hide her and keep her safe while we fight."

"Listen to me, Gray. Please. You're not hearing me. I know Tammen and I know Granger. It was bad enough that I rejected my chosen male. I insulted not only Brent, but my father, as well. Even if they don't try to kill all of you, they're definitely going to make an example of me."

Micah's wolf had been settled since he'd marked Callie, even if he was constantly pining for her, obsessing over her, chattering in Micah's head to be near her. But now, he was pushing forward and trying to take Micah's body. He gritted his teeth and clenched his fists. He needed to move. He needed to pace.

Jumping to his feet, Micah jumped from the porch onto the ground and rolled his head, cracking his neck. He could feel the vibrations rolling through his body as he fought the Shift. He needed to keep his head, he needed to be there for Callie, but if his wolf took over, he knew he'd lose all control. This was what he'd been trying to avoid since she'd come onto their land. This was what he'd feared from day one.

Even now, as he searched her eyes, he could see her confusion shining in her golden eyes. She narrowed them and a little crease developed between her brows.

"Micah?" she said, unfolding her legs and lifting onto her knees. "What's wrong? What are you doing?"

She stood and took a step forward. He lifted his hand and shook his head. He needed her to stay back, even though his wolf was trying to force his feet closer to her. If he Shifted now, he knew he'd lose all control of his actions.

"Micah, calm down, brother," Gray said. His Alpha knew Micah's wolf was unsteady, even if he never said a word about it. He took a step closer to Micah, his hands held out in front of him. "Calm your wolf, Micah."

"I'm trying," he forced through clenched teeth. "Callie, please go inside." She shook her head, but that crease was gone. "Please," he said, but his voice was no longer his own. *Shit. Please don't hurt her*, he begged his wolf.

Callie. Mine. Mate.

Instead of turning and going into her house like Micah had hoped, Callie slowly stepped down each step, the wood creaking under her weight, until she stood barely a foot from him. "Micah," she whispered, reaching up to cup his face. He jerked away and there was a flash of hurt in her eyes. But she didn't turn away from him, didn't back off. "Wolf," she said, making her voice stronger.

"Callie," Emory called out as she jogged over. "Back up."

"Oh, shit," Reed said from Micah's left. More footsteps, more mumbling around him. His whole Pack was nearby now, ready to step in if Micah lost himself and went after Gray...or Callie.

No. That would never happen. Even as fear for her safety burned at the back of his brain, his wolf was more focused on finding Brent and ending the threat to Micah's mate, to his wolf's mate.

"Please, Callie," Micah ground out as the first wave of pain hit him and nausea rolled his stomach. He was fighting the Shift and his wolf was fighting back just as hard. He dropped to his hands and knees and grunted as his bones snapped and reshaped.

"Shiiiiit," Reed said before an echoing set of snapping bones filled the air. Was Reed Shifting, or was it someone else?

Micah didn't know and couldn't focus on anything but trying to get through his Shift without injuring a member of his own Pack. Within seconds, although it felt like hours, he stood on four paws, shaking his dark gray fur out.

Callie closed the distance between them and ran her fingers through the rough hair along his neck.

"Kitty, back up. What are you doing?" Nova said, mild panic in her voice.

"Don't you dare come any closer," Gray said, pointing a finger at his mate. His eyes dropped back to Micah. "Change back, Second," he said, putting as much power as he could into his order.

But his wolf was no longer interested in paying attention to his Alpha. He was no longer interested in taking orders from anyone. He had one thing and one thing only on his mind...find and kill Brent.

∞ ∞ ∞

Callie's heart was going crazy in her chest, but she knew with every fiber of her being that Micah wouldn't hurt her, and that included his wolf. The top of his head was over a foot taller than her and his shoulders reached hers, even as she stood beside him. He was beautiful. She'd never been so close to a wolf Shifter in this form. Had never felt the immense amount of power rolling from a Shifter as she did at that moment.

With trembling hands, she reached forward and thread her fingers through the fur at his neck. He turned his head and almost leaned into her touch. Just as she'd thought, his wolf knew her. He recognized his mate.

"What is he doing?" Nova screeched out, but Tristan pulled her away as Gray jabbed a finger in her direction again. Why did she keep trying to move closer if everyone was obviously so worried about Micah's sudden Shift?

"Stay back, Nova. It's fine," Callie said, dropping her hand from Micah's scruff.

Micah lowered his head until they were lined up eye to eye. What was going through his mind? She had a feeling she knew what caused him to go unhinged, but what was his wolf thinking now?

Taking a step back, Micah lifted his snout in the air and sniffed, his head turning toward the West.

"Micah, stop," Callie said, reaching for him again.

He glanced at her and took another step back. Oh no. He was going hunting. He was going to challenge Brent. But what he didn't realize was how many lions he'd have to go through to get to him.

"Please, stop. Don't do this," she begged.

Another step back. And another. He turned and took off like a bullet. Gray yelled, dropped to his knees and Shifted, his clothes exploding and falling to the ground like confetti. Tristan and Reed were chasing him now, too.

She couldn't let this happen. She couldn't let him fight. She couldn't let him die.

Opening her mouth, she released a scream that tapered into a roar as she let her lioness have her body. She was running the second her paws slammed into the hard ground.

Emory watched with wide eyes, standing close to Nova, as Callie joined the chase. The wolves were lithe and much bigger than she was, but she was faster. While the lions were strong and charged with protecting the females, the lionesses were naturally the hunters. It was their job in the wild to bring back the food. She wasn't fully lion, but she wasn't fully human, either.

Dust kicked up around her as she pushed hard, her nails digging into the dry ground. A few more feet. She was so close. If they didn't catch him, he'd make it too close to the highway and risk being seen by humans. Was his wolf insane? Did he have no survival instincts? If he exposed them to the human population, he'd be imprisoned or executed, and he couldn't use the excuse of ignorance as Nova had.

Callie passed Reed, then Tristan, and even Gray. Her muscles burned as she forced them to work harder. The breath was coming from her mouth in rough pants. And then she reached out a paw and swiped at Micah's back leg.

She caught his flesh in one of her claws and yanked. She knew she'd cut him, knew he'd be injured, but it stopped him. He stumbled, then rolled ass over nose until he settled in a cloud of dust.

He whirled on her, his teeth bared, a snarl deep in his throat.

She swiped at him again, screeching and hissing. *Come on, Micah. Push your wolf back.*

A few more seconds of a stare down and Micah's ears flattened to his head and he whined. He sat back and licked at the claw mark on his hind leg. When he looked back up at her, Callie tilted her head in confusion. He was in wolf form, yet his eyes were flashing back and forth between their human blue-green and his wolf's bright icy blue.

She wanted to speak to him but worried if she Shifted back, he'd just take off again. She really, really didn't want to have to cause real damage to him, but she would if it kept him safe. He lifted his head and scented the air again, but when he stood, he favored the leg she'd ripped in her claws. With a chuff, he sat back onto his haunches and watched her as if waiting for something. What, she didn't know. Gray grunted as he turned back into man and pointed a finger at Micah.

"Fucking Shift back," he roared at him, his eyes still bright blue with anger.

Micah flopped onto his belly and writhed on the ground as his bones slowly snapped and reshaped. He sat naked on his hands and knees, his calf oozing blood as he gasped for air. "Fuck," he mumbled under his breath. Rolling onto his back, he stared up into the sky while he struggled for breath. "Fuck." This time, his words were louder.

Callie looked to Gray, who nodded at her. She Shifted back and knelt beside Micah, but Tristan and Reed stayed in their wolf forms, standing over her, standing sentry just in case. She didn't bother to hide her nudity, felt no embarrassment over the men staring down at her as she tried to coax Micah to a sitting position.

"I've fucked everything up for you," he said, his voice full of pain, both physical and emotional.

"No, you haven't. You've given me everything."

Micah rolled his head and looked at her. "I was selfish and wanted to keep you. I knew what would happen. I knew you were claimed. Knew we were breaking your fucking laws. I knew my wolf wasn't stable enough for this. I knew I couldn't control him. Yet I took everything from you, marked you, and now..." His eyes slammed closed, but not before Callie saw the shimmer of moisture there.

"You didn't cause this. They did. The lions did. They're the ones who tried to take everything from me. What we did? What you did? It was perfect and unavoidable. You said you didn't regret it. Or did that change?"

His head lifted and Callie smiled. The back of his hair was matted with sweat, dirt, and grass. Brushing the debris from his hair, she kept her eyes averted from his face. There was already so much rushing through her; she didn't need to see the pain in his eyes, too.

"Of course, it didn't change."

"Then shut up," she said, finally looking at him. "Alan said he'll do what he can to fix this. He has a daughter. Other members of the council have daughters. We just have to appeal to their sense of parental love."

When she'd gotten home, her entire world felt like it was crashing down around her. She couldn't see any light at the top of the chasm she'd fallen into. And maybe she still felt that same despair, but she couldn't take the fact Micah was more or less blaming himself.

There wasn't a whole lot she could do, had literally no control of her own life, but at least here, with these people, with Micah, she felt like it was her life. She felt like she had a fighting chance.

Helping Micah to his feet, she shook her head when Gray took a step forward. Yeah, the news had obviously riled up her mate, but there was so much more going on. It wasn't a natural response to their conversation. Even for someone with an unstable animal. She was tired of him holding back information, always finding ways to distract her.

Tristan and Reed Shifted back to their human forms and Callie kept her eyes averted from their swinging schlongs as they walked back to the houses with her. It was obvious they didn't trust Micah's wolf to refrain from once again taking Micah's body. They made sure he went home, even stood off to the side as Callie led him into his house.

He needed to get dressed. He needed to sit down and he needed to finally open up to her.

"Here," she said, tossing him a pair of jeans from on top of his dresser. They hadn't spent nearly as much time in his house as they did hers, and it was obvious by the mess left everywhere. With his place being so small, even a cup in the sink made everything look cluttered. But at least it finally looked lived in and a little homier.

Her eyes moved to the beige and green striped curtains, the only personal touch to his place. "Where'd you get those?" she asked with a jerk of her chin as he pulled his pants up his legs.

He turned and looked over his shoulder to where she was gesturing. "Nova."

Crossing the small space, she ran her fingers down the fabric and frowned at a frayed spot toward the end. It looked like someone had ripped it with their teeth or claws. "She got you curtains?"

"She likes to buy gifts. When she was still pretty new here, she snuck in one day and hung those." He was staring at the curtains as if he was conjuring the memory. "Pissed Gray off."

"That what happened here?" she asked, pointing to the torn area.

He dipped his head once. "Came home from work and he scented her in my place. Freaked out, yanked them down, and was ready to beat my ass over them."

"Why?" She released the curtain and leaned against the wall. "Why would he beat your ass over that?"

"He thought she'd come into my house, which she had. But it was when they were still newly mated. He was all possessive and shit and would get pissed when anyone even looked at Nova."

Callie raised one brow.

"Yeah, I know. Same way." He sat on his couch and dragged a hand down his face. "I'm so fucking sorry."

Callie pushed from the wall and went to sit next to her mate. "For what?"

"You could've gotten hurt, Callie. Don't come that close when my wolf takes my body."

She narrowed her eyes and let them wander across his face. "You don't have much control over him, do you?" He shook his head. "Did he make you mark me?"

He jerked his head around to stare at her wide-eyed. "No. I mean, yeah. He wanted you pretty fucking badly, but that was all me. I fucked you and I marked you. He just went fucking crazy when I did…crazier."

"Micah…" She pulled her eyes from his face. "Talk to me."

It was his turn to look away. "I haven't even told Gray everything," he admitted barely above a whisper.

"Are you worried what he'll think?"

He shook his head. "No… it's just…fuck," he muttered, then dropped his head into his hands, gripping his hair and pulling. She tried to pull his hands away before he yanked his hair out by the roots, but he jerked away from her. "Please don't touch me. Not now."

Well, that stung a bit.

Callie pulled away and turned on the couch so her left knee was pointed at him and waited for him to talk. She wasn't going to drop this. Whatever secret Micah carried affected them every day. Hell, had she not caught up to him, he might have already outed them to the humans or made it to Tammen territory. He'd be dead and she'd be nothing but a shell.

"I had a sister," he finally blurted out after about ten minutes of some kind of internal struggle.

"Had," she whispered into the quiet room.

"Had. As in, I don't anymore. She's dead."

"I'm so sorry," Callie said, reaching for him then dropping her arm when he jerked away again.

"We grew up in a Pack way too fucking much like Tammen. They didn't live by even a resemblance of a moral code. They took what they wanted, when they wanted. If someone got in their way, they'd just attack them as a Pack. If they survived, they'd usually run off. If they died..." He shrugged. "Just as good. Either way, they were out of the way of the Alpha. My dad."

Whoa. His dad had been Alpha of his Pack. "Who was your Pack?"

"Latran," he answered.

That didn't make sense. "I thought Latran were a Pack of coyotes."

"They were. Until my dad moved in and bred them out. My mom was a coyote Shifter. I'm not fully wolf."

That actually explained a lot about his animal's instability. Coyote Shifters were known to be out of control, constantly fighting their own Pack for one reason or another. They fought over hunting, they fought over territory, they fought because the sun was up or down. They were violent and terrifying and half nuts.

"Your dad didn't accept you guys," she guessed.

He shook his head. "It was one thing to have a son who was a half-breed. It was another to have a daughter of breeding age he couldn't make much money from."

Callie's stomach turned. Just like the men from the lion Prides, his own dad sold off females, including his own daughter. "What happened?"

Micah lunged to his feet suddenly, startling Callie. She flinched back and watched as he paced from one wall to the other, his hands clenching into fists then relaxing. "Callie, I can't—"

"You can," she interrupted him before he could put this off any longer. He had to get it out of him. He had to share the secret with someone else, let her share his burden, let her carry some of the weight of whatever happened in his past.

A growl was trickling from him and his eyes were icy blue. He'd glance at her, then his gaze would dart away. He did this over and over until she put her other foot on the ground and faced him fully.

"Micah, look at me. Nothing you can say will make me change the way I feel about you."

He huffed out a sarcastic laugh. "Yeah," he muttered more to himself.

"Just say it. Say it quickly."

"I couldn't save her," he blurted out, finally making eye contact with her. His animal was close; she could see it in his eyes, the way he was shaking, and could smell his fur.

"Your sister?"

He gripped his hair again, then entwined his fingers on the top of his head. "Yeah. My little sister. She was only sixteen."

Just like Callie had been when she'd been delivered to Tammen. "What happened?"

Micah's shoulders shook as if he were holding in a sob. "She was supposed to be sold to Deathport."

Holy shit. More and more was clicking into place. "Anson?"

"Fucking Anson," he said. "She was beautiful. Even so young, you could see the woman she'd be one day." He glanced up at her and she saw the shimmer of tears again. "She was so fucking smart. And funny. And mouthy as hell. I was there when my dad told her she'd be going to live with Deathport. I've never heard so many cuss words come from one person's mouth in my life." He laughed a huffed sound then smiled through his tears. "She was supposed to be Anson's mate. She argued with my dad, told him to fuck off. I had her back. I was only eighteen, but I had her fucking back. Hell, Anson was only eighteen at the time, too. Who knew if he really wanted the pairing or was just doing what his Alpha ordered?"

"What happened, Micah?" Callie whispered, afraid to make her voice any louder for fear of breaking his pace. It was like he was reliving that moment as he told the story.

"Deathport came for her. A few of us stood our ground, tired of the bullshit, tired of our sisters and friends being sold off. There was this huge fight. Even the women fought." A tear trailed down his cheek and he didn't bother to wipe it away. "She was killed."

He dropped to his knees like his legs wouldn't hold him up anymore. "There were three wolves trying to maneuver her to their car and she snapped her fangs at them, fought them. I was trying to get to her side, trying to help her get away from them. But even members of our own fucking pack, my own fucking *dad* was fighting against me. I turned around and Deathport's Alpha had his teeth latched around her fucking throat. He said he was just trying to claim her; mark her so she didn't have a choice. She bled out on the fucking ground, right in front of me, and there wasn't a thing I could do to stop it." He looked at his hands as if he could still see his sister's blood there. Finally, he raised his eyes to hers, the icy blue gone, tears streaming down his face one after another. "My dad blamed me. Said if I'd just done what I was supposed to do she'd be alive. He exiled me. I was an eighteen-year-old kid and he exiled me. I was alone, pissed, and scared. A couple years later, I came across Gray and his brother. The next thing you know, Reed, then Emory and Tristan joined us and we became a Pack. They've all grown and created these cool lives, and I'm still stuck. I'm broken."

"What was her name?" Callie whispered.

His eyes widened slightly and he looked a little surprised. "Heather."

Callie scooted from the couch and knelt in front of him, taking both of his hands in hers. "Micah, you're not broken. Your heart is, but you've created a really cool life, too. You have this amazing Pack. You're Second in command; that's pretty damn impressive. You're strong and loyal. And you're an amazing mate. You're not broken. Just a little lost."

More tears streaked down his face. How did none of his Pack know about his history? How had he carried this with him all these years and not snapped? "I think you should tell Gray."

He raised his head and looked at her, his brows pulled together, his eyes red-rimmed. "Why?"

"Because he's your friend. He's your family. It could help you guys be closer and help him understand you a little more."

He dropped his head again and shook it. She wouldn't push him on this. If and when he decided to share the worst moment of his life with anyone from the Pack it would be on his time. When it felt right. When he felt stronger.

For now, she'd carry this for him, help him grieve it so he could honor Heather's memory, not through vengeance, but by living the life she would've wanted.

Callie wrapped her arms around his neck and held him close, just being there for him as he released eight years' worth of emotions. He sobbed softly on her shoulder, his warm tears soaking through her shirt and clung to her as if she were his lifeline. She wasn't sure how long they sat like that, holding each other on the hardwood floor. Time didn't matter. What mattered was she could almost feel Micah's heart mending piece by piece. She could almost feel his animal calming. She could feel everything he didn't say in the way his arms stayed tight around her back.

When he was all cried out, he pulled from her and scrubbed his hands over his face. "Fuck. Now I'm exhausted," he said with a half-smile.

"Yeah. Crying takes a lot out of you." She reached forward and gently wiped away a tear he'd missed with her fingertips. "But you always feel a little better after."

"A little." He sniffled. "I've never cried over Heather. Even after she died, I just...I don't know, bottled it up, I guess. I didn't want to accept she was gone, and I felt like if I grieved her..." He shrugged.

"She is gone. But she'll never be forgotten. She's in your heart, and now she's in mine. And we'll build a life together in her honor. We'll have the kids she never had the chance to birth. We'll love enough for two lifetimes."

Another tear escaped over his lashes, but this time, it was with a soft smile, the kind that melts a heart. "Thank you," he whispered.

Chapter Eight

The next Saturday, Callie was on edge as she waited for Nova's dad.

"It'll be fine," Nova told her as they sat on her and Gray's front porch.

Callie forced a smile and continued to watch for Alan's grey sedan to come down the long driveway. He'd met with the council. He had news. That was all he'd tell them on the phone. That could be good news or bad news, and Callie really wasn't a fan of suspense.

Micah leaned against the porch, his arms crossed over his chest. He watched her closely, his eyes occasionally taking on his wolf's icy blue before fading to his normal color. It was unnerving at times how much his animal controlled her mate, how often he watched Callie, how close he was to the surface all the time. He'd settled a little after Micah had opened up to her, but the uncertainty hanging over their heads was getting to him just as much as it was her.

Reed and Tristan wandered over, their brows furrowed, their lips pressed into grim lines. At least she wasn't the only one terrified of the outcome. What if Alan said the council ruled against her? Then what? She wouldn't go back. She *couldn't* go back. She knew exactly what would happen to her the second she was in Tammen territory again.

But, if the council deemed Callie and Micah law breakers, would she have much of a choice? Even more concerning, what would happen to Micah? Nova had been acquitted of her crimes because she literally had no idea there *were* laws. While Callie had been a little fuzzy on her facts, it had seemed Micah was fully aware she wasn't free to be marked or mated. She'd been claimed with her father's blessing and he'd taken what Brent saw as his property.

She'd been worth no more than the car she'd stolen the night she'd run away. No. That wasn't true. She was worth less. She was just a portal for more cubs. Reed had said Trever did a circle around his car, checking for any dents or dings when he'd met him at Moe's, but didn't ask how Callie was doing, just whether she was going to make things easier on all of them.

Easier for who? Not for Micah. Not for her new Pack. And definitely not for Callie.

Chewing the inside of her cheek, her stomach flipped and her heart picked up its pace as the grey sedan came into view. From where she sat, she could see two heads in the front of the car. And two trucks were following close behind.

As they all pulled alongside the Pack's trucks, Nova pushed to her feet with a grunt and joined Gray and the others as they moved to welcome Colton, Carter, Luke, and Noah. If Noah was there, who was manning the bar? And did that mean Alan had really bad news that the entire Clan felt like they needed to be there when he delivered the verdict?

With shaky knees, Callie climbed to her feet and waited as they all turned and stared at her, their eyes wide...and smiles on all of their faces.

"What?" she breathed out when Nova waddled, both hands wrapped around the bottom of her stomach, to where Callie waited to hear her fate.

Micah had stayed beside her while the rest of them had greeted Carter, Alan, and the others. She could feel the tension rolling from him, could sense his wolf close to the surface, could smell his fur. He wrapped a hand around hers, pulled her close, and waited.

"Hey, girl," Colton said, stretching his arms toward her for a hug, then pulling them back when Micah snarled. "Down, boy. Just ready to celebrate."

With deep breaths, Callie tried to slow her heart rate as Alan walked directly to her, stopping within a couple of feet.

"Good news, Callie."

Good news. *Okay, heart. Slow down before I pass out in front of everyone.*

Gray led everyone to the circle of lawn chairs around the firepit and helped his mate into her chair. Micah pulled his chair until it was pressed against Callie's and held her hand tightly as they waited for everyone to get comfortable.

"For fuck's sake," Micah barked out. "Just spit it out. What's the deal?"

Alan didn't seem fazed. Neither did Colton's father, Frank. They both smiled at each other then turned to Callie.

"Turns out not all lions are sick bastards," Frank said. "We were able to talk to the surrounding councils. There were sixty-three elders who voted. It was forty-one to twenty-two. The laws will be revisited."

"What does that even mean? Revisited, how?" Nova said, a frown between her brows.

Alan smiled at his daughter. "It seems we aren't the only ones who feel the law is ridiculous. Even some of the lion elders believe it's beyond time to join the twenty-first century. Women aren't property. There were some who disagreed, but they were outnumbered. When we leave here, we'll deliver the verdict to Tammen and Granger. Until the law has been rewritten, all those women are considered free. They can choose to leave, with their cubs, or they can choose to stay in that lifestyle."

"And after the law is rewritten?" Callie asked. She couldn't believe this was happening. They'd done it. They'd fought and won.

"What do you mean?" Alan asked.

"You said until the law is rewritten. What about after?" Callie asked.

Alan leaned forward, his elbows on his knees. "We'll have to have another meeting to determine how exactly the law will be rewritten."

"It sounds more like there's just a break in the slavery of women until further notice," Emory said. Her voice was full of the same tension the rest of them felt.

"There will still have to be laws about mated females."

"That should be the woman's choice," Gray said. "If she wants to leave for another male, that should be up to her."

"Agreed. We still have to protect everyone, though. Even though the laws are changing, there is still a long way to go. There will be a lot of backlash, I promise you that. These Packs and Prides who trick women into their territory, or even the ones like the Prides who forced their daughters into unwanted pairings, aren't going to want this change. They're going to do everything they can, find every loophole possible to claim unmated females. A marked or mated female is off limits, even in their own minds. We have to give something to persuade the twenty-two to compromise," Frank said.

"Bullshit," Colton said, taking off his black hat and setting it on his knee.

"Yeah, what Colton said. Bullshit," Nova said.

"For now, let's consider this a victory. Callie is free to stay with Micah. She's free to stay with the Big River Pack. All those lionesses are free to stay or go."

"Until another group of men decide otherwise?" Emory asked. "What about unmated females?"

"What about them?" Alan asked.

"Are we still considered up for grabs?"

"You're free unless a male can convince you into a pairing," Alan said.

"Convince me?" Emory asked, and then her eyes flashed to blue.

"She was already free," Reed said, his voice full of venom.

"Technically. Unless a male claimed her," Frank said. He held up his hands, palms out, when growling erupted around the circle. "At no point was rape or kidnapping legal. But if a male could convince a female to mate..." He shrugged.

"Convince. Like bartering for one's freedom over the other?" Gray asked.

Deathport had blackmailed Gray and the rest of Big River when Nova had arrived. They'd wanted Emory in their Pack, they'd wanted to breed her, wanted her to pop out more pups for their numbers. They'd negotiated; they wouldn't turn Nova over to the council if Big River gave them Emory. Then, Tammen had more or less used the same page in their playbook, pretending to be willing to let Callie and the fact she and Micah had broken a law go if they'd hand over Emory.

The poor woman couldn't get a break.

"So, you mean, if they can successfully threaten or manipulate me into allowing them to mark me," Emory said. Unlike the guys, Emory was always calm. But not now. Now, her wolf was right there. Her eyes were bright blue and she trembled slightly as she fought a Shift.

"This is a good thing, guys. I know you don't see it that way, but it is. It's the first step in changing everything," Frank said, his eyes bouncing to each person in the circle, including his own son. "You have to trust us. You have to trust the council."

Callie pulled her bottom lip into her mouth and worried it. It wasn't a done deal yet, but Frank was right. This was the first step in a long process. Who knew how long it would take for the surrounding councils to meet again to rewrite the laws?

For now, lionesses were free. *She* was free. But...

"What about Micah?" Callie asked. "What about Rhett's accusations against him?"

Alan nodded. "He did break their law. But, since the law has been overturned until further notice, we're going to overlook his slight."

"It wasn't a fucking slight," Micah said.

Callie tightened her hand around his and looked up at him. She smiled softly and tried to calm him. "We're free," she said softly. Her smile spread. "You're free. I'm free. All female Shifters are free."

"Holy shit," Nova muttered. "We did it?" Alan winked at his daughter. "Suffragettes win again!" She pumped a fist into the air with a *whoop*.

"Seriously. You need to do a little more research," Reed said, but there was a smile on his face. He was relaxing. Everyone was.

As if someone flipped a switch, the collective mood changed. Even Micah loosened his grip on her hand.

"When do you go see Rhett?" Gray asked.

Nova, Emory, Colton, Luke, and Tristan were up and moving around. Colton carried over a big cooler while Tristan and Luke helped the girls carry a crap ton of food from the back of Colton's truck. It was cookout time. It was celebration time.

"Tomorrow," Alan answered. He turned in his seat as a few more trucks rumbled down the drive.

Gray raised his hand in greeting. Ravenwood was joining them.

"Well?" Aron asked as he rushed over. "What happened?"

"How did you even know they were here?" Gray asked.

Nova called out from where she was trying to figure out how to light the grill. "I texted them. Duh."

"Hey, preggo," Aron called out. "Does she know what she's doing?" he asked as he watched her bend over and study the knobs on the grill.

Gray turned and looked behind him. "Babe, hold on." He jogged over to her and showed her how to work the grill.

Callie just sat there and watched everyone interacting, watched as Ravenwood shook hands or hugged their greetings. She had this big, funny, sometimes intimidating family and they'd fought and won. For her. For lionesses. For women everywhere.

How had she gotten here? Just a few weeks ago she was fantasizing about a different life, a life where she wasn't subjected to Brent's blows, a life where she didn't listen to the soft sobs from the lionesses trapped in that existence.

And now, she was living her fantasy.

Nope. Not even close. She could've never dreamed life could be this good. She could've never believed she'd grow to love so many people or be loved right back.

"What are you smiling about?" Micah asked. He stood and grabbed two beers from the cooler and handed her one after popping the top.

"We did it, Micah. That's it. No more worrying, no more anxiety, no more fear."

He didn't look convinced. Just nodded as she spoke, his eyes unfocused as he stared into the woods across their property. *Their* property. It was hers, too. She had a home of her own, a mate, and a Pack. It wasn't the way she'd imagined it, but it was perfect.

"They still have to take the news back to Tammen," Micah said, returning his eyes to her face.

"You're killing the mood, Micah," Nova called from the grill as she pointed a spatula at him.

Micah grinned a tight-lipped smile at her and nodded.

"What are you worried about? The council has final say. We're free, mate," Callie said when he turned back to her.

She knew what he was worried about, but didn't want to discuss the possibility of Tammen and possibly Granger going after not just Big River, but the members of the council, as well. The council members were Shifters, just like her, but they were older. Some of them were in their late sixties and even seventies. They were easy targets.

And what if the Prides went after the council members' families, their daughters and sisters to prove a point?

Nope. She wasn't thinking about that right now. They weren't discussing it. For now, they were going to celebrate the victory and pretend everything would stay as perfect as it was in that moment.

"How much food did you guys bring?" Emory asked as Colton carried over a few more plastic bags.

"There are a lot of us. And I'm hungry," he answered, pulling out bags of chips and containers of potato salad and cole slaw from the little grocery store down the road. "Besides, Nova's eating for two. Gotta make sure Wolfgang is fed."

"See? He gets it," Nova said from the grill. "Ouch." She yanked her hand away and studied it.

"Oh, for fuck's sake," Micah grumbled and stood. He stomped over to the grill and gently pushed Nova away, waving Gray off when he tried to take over. "I got it."

Nova had a wide smile as she waddled back to the chairs. "I figured he'd have taken over the second I couldn't figure out the stupid knobs."

Callie shook her head and smiled back, winking at Micah when he gave her a look that said he knew exactly what Nova had been up to. He seemed more at ease with a job to do, so Callie sat back and listened to the group of men and two women.

"I'm just saying, if a female Shifter was President, Shifters would be out to the public, legal, and none of this crap would be going on," Nova said.

"If a woman was President, men would be locked up every time she went through PMS," Reed said with a snort.

"You're a dork," Emory said, pulling her legs up onto her chair and tucking them beneath herself.

Tristan leaned over and whispered something in Emory's ear. Her brows lowered and she nodded. Callie watched them, studied them, and couldn't help but wonder about their relationship, about their connection. Tristan rarely said more than two words, was content standing silently on the sideline, but it was obvious he cared about Emory. It was obvious he cared about the entire Pack. He was loyal to them. But there was definitely a stronger bond between him and Emory.

"Are you guys related?" Callie asked, then instantly felt like an idiot.

They didn't resemble each other, unless you counted the blue eyes and dark hair. Emory was tiny, not standing more than five-foot-one or two. She had big, round, beautiful eyes and an angular face with high cheekbones and a thin body. Her hair was so dark auburn it almost appeared black until the light hit it.

Tristan was close to six-foot-two, had broad shoulders, and a square jaw with a little cleft in his chin. His eyes were a darker blue than Emory's turquoise.

Emory snorted. "No."

"You guys do act pretty close," Colton said with his brows raised. "Can we expect another declaration of mates soon?"

In a very uncharacteristic move, Tristan widened his eyes and shook his head. "Uh, no," he said, probably using up his daily allowance of words.

"Then what's the deal?" Colton asked, standing and reaching into the cooler for another beer. "Seems like the only person he talks to is you," he said to Emory with a raised brow. "You two showed up together and are always connected at the hip."

"That's not true. I hang out with Reed the most," Emory protested.

Colton continued to smirk at her with raised brows.

"We're not mates. Just friends. And, yeah, we came together, but the rest is none of your business," she told Colton, crossing her arms and pursing her lips.

Callie wanted to know just as bad as everyone else watching them, but she really didn't want to be the person to piss Emory off, either.

Hoping to get the attention off Emory, Callie turned to Alan. "How did you find out you were Nova's dad?" she asked then winked at Emory when the conversation began to flow about anything and everything except Emory's past.

Alan told the story of how he'd met Nova's mom when they were younger, about how he'd left when things got too serious. He didn't want to have to tell her about Shifters. He wasn't sure whether he could trust her with a secret that big, and didn't want the chance of it freaking her out.

Lo and behold, even though he'd tried to protect her, he'd had no idea she was pregnant. It wasn't until Nova got on the council's radar that he began to poke around. It was rare for a Shifter to be living in the city, and even rarer for an unmated female to live without a Pack or a mate.

"But what happened to her?" Emory asked. "What happened to her mom?"

"That's for Nova to disclose," Alan said, leaning back and crossing his ankle over his knee.

This was the first time other than breakfast Callie had ever hung out with anyone from the Shifter council. If they were all as laid back and caring as Frank and Alan, the chances of the laws being completely overturned, including those regarding unmated females, were a lot greater.

"But, did you find her? Does she know where Nova is?" Emory asked, prodding further.

Callie leaned forward a little. She was curious, too.

"He did. No; she doesn't know where I am. And, no, I haven't contacted her," Nova said, her eyes on the cold firepit. It was still too warm of an afternoon for a fire.

"You don't want to talk to her?" Callie asked.

Nova shrugged, just a slight movement of her shoulders. "Maybe someday after Wolfgang's born. Not now, though. I mean, come on. She deserted me. I was just a kid. The least she could've done was dropped me off at the zoo when I Shifted. Instead, she dumped me in the street like a stray dog." Nova's eyes glistened and she blinked them rapidly, trying to clear them before they trailed down her cheek. "Whatever. Her loss. 'Cause I'm a pretty cool ass daughter. Right, Dad?" she asked, smiling wide at Alan. But Callie could see how forced that smile was and how hard she was trying to pretend everything was fine.

Yet another conversation with too many open wounds. Maybe she should toss Micah's sister in the conversation and see if she couldn't fully upset everyone in one fell swoop.

"Hey, Callie," Colton said, breaking into her internal self-abuse. "Now that you're free to marry whoever the hell you want, when are you and Micah going to give us some pups?"

"She could have cubs, Colton," Nova said, accepting a bottle of sweet tea from Alan.

"Either way. I'm ready for a bunch of kids running around here."

"You going to change all their diapers and send them all to college?" Nova asked.

"I'll babysit, but I don't know about diapers."

Callie's cheeks heated as the attention was turned on her and Micah. "Oh. I don't know. Not for a while."

"You could just do like me and Gray and totally not plan it. It's more fun. Like Christmas morning in the middle of the year," Nova said.

And now her cheeks were even hotter. It wasn't that she was embarrassed talking about starting a family, exactly. It was the way one started a family that was getting to her. She really didn't want to talk about her sex life with all these people.

"Hey, Callie?" Micah called from the grill. She turned and looked at him over the top of her chair. "Want to get married?"

She blinked at him. Then blinked again. Her mouth slowly fell open as she stared at her mate.

"Did you just propose to her while holding tongs?" Reed asked as he chuckled. "We're a romantic bunch, aren't we?"

"Okay. We're totally planning a big wedding for you two," Nova said.

"Maybe she wants one like you had," Emory argued.

But Callie just continued to stare at Micah.

"Are you going to answer?" Reed asked, standing and nudging her with his beer bottle.

She glanced at Reed then turned back to Micah. "Um…yes?"

"Is that a yes, you'll answer, or yes, you want to get married?" Reed asked.

"Dude, shut up and let her think. She looks a little freaked out right now," Gray said, but there was obvious amusement in his voice.

"Yes, I want to get married?" She wasn't really sure how to answer this. He hadn't exactly asked her if she wanted to marry *him*. Just asked if she wanted to get married. So, the honest answer was that she did, indeed, want to get married. Someday. To Micah.

"I'm ordained," Aron from Ravenwood blurted out with his hand in the air.

"We don't need that," Micah said. "Not like we're going to a church."

"Can we please have a big wedding this time?" Emory asked.

"*We* aren't getting married. *They* are," Reed said.

"Yeah, but – "

"Callie," Micah barked out over all the noise and silenced the back and forth bickering. "Wanna marry me?" He'd set down the tongs this time, but still stood at least ten feet away, manning the grill.

"Micah," she said, trying to arrange her thoughts into a coherent sentence. "I thought we were already kind of married."

"I want to see you in a white dress like Nova wore. I want to say pretty things to you and watch you smile."

"I—"

What the hell did she say to that? She wanted to do anything and everything to make him happy. But a wedding just so he could see her in a gown? Just so he could recite vows to her? It wasn't like their marriage would be legally accepted anywhere. It wasn't like they could go to the courthouse and get a marriage certificate. Shifters did everything they could to stay off the radar of any human government. Their utilities were under an alias, they didn't have credit cards or loans, everything they bought was with cash.

That is, until Nova came along and turned everything on its head. She was the first Shifter Callie had ever heard of who was in the public eye and even had a bank account in her real name.

Where Nova had naivete on her side, both Callie and Micah knew a wedding would be nothing more than symbolic.

Micah finally abandoned the grill and made his way over to her. He offered his hand and pulled her from the chair, guiding her away from the group a little. He gripped both her hands in his and actually dropped to one knee.

"Micah, stop," she whispered, trying to tug him up. This was too much. It was all too much. "Can we talk about this later?"

As if he just realized they had an audience and that he was making her really uncomfortable with all the attention, he blinked fast and stood up even faster. "Oh, yeah. Sorry."

What the hell had gotten into him? She'd seen more emotion from him when he'd told her about Heather than she had the entire time she'd been with the Pack. Unless she counted all the times she'd seen him either angry or extremely passionate.

Now he was ready to more or less propose marriage to her in front of all their friends.

"Well, that was awkward," Reed said. Micah glared at him and Reed shrunk down a little. "Sorry. Just kidding."

He was right, though. It was way awkward. Time to once again try to change subjects. It felt like she'd been backpedaling or trying to redirect the spotlight since Alan and Frank had arrived.

"Is the food ready?" she asked, smiling up at Micah.

He returned her smile, but his eyes didn't crinkle at the edges. Well, shit. He was disappointed by her refusal to answer or maybe by her refusal to allow him to properly propose. It just didn't seem genuine, or like it was really rushed. She wanted him, forever, but she didn't want him to decide on a whim he was ready for marital bliss.

Micah returned to the grill and began lifting pieces of meat from the fire and placing them on a huge pan. The guys jumped up and shoved each other out of the way as they tried to get first pick.

"Back off, fuckers," Micah growled out, crossing his arms and creating a barricade to the food. "Nova first. Then the girls."

"Yeah," Gray said, pushing to the front and making two plates.

Callie and Emory smiled at each other and hurried to grab what they wanted before the guys decimated the selection. Callie had never been a big eater, but she was hungry and Micah could grill like no one's business.

Once everyone's plates were filled, they all sat around in a circle, eating, talking, joking, just enjoying the evening. No doubt the fact

Alan was taking the news to Tammen and Granger the next day was on everyone's minds, but no one brought it up. There was no use obsessing over something they had no control over. They'd just have to wait and see what happened tomorrow.

∞ ∞ ∞

What the fuck was he thinking? Yeah, he wanted to spend the next sixty plus years with Callie, but why the hell had he thought blurting that shit out in front of every single person they knew was a good idea? She'd looked like someone had kicked her fucking dog or something.

He watched her interact with the Pack, with the guys from Blackwater and Ravenwood. She'd grown so much in the short time since she'd come there. Micah could still see her fighting to refrain from retreating back into herself when it came to her own needs, but she had no problem expressing herself. She laughed and joked and hardly cast her eyes down anymore when she felt she was out of place or had asked too personal a question.

She hadn't accepted his proposal. She hadn't exactly rejected him, but she'd definitely been shocked by his outburst. He was such an idiot. Always fucking this all up one way or another. For some reason, he thought if he threw marriage out there, she'd jump up and down with a smile and a tear in her eye. He pictured her standing in front of him with a gorgeous white gown, her blonde hair all curled up, and crying as he spewed some poetic shit.

Yeah, because he was real poetic. He couldn't even propose correctly. At least he'd remembered to drop to one knee, even if he hadn't thought about a ring…or, you know, what exactly he was doing. It was just there, in his head, and he'd said it.

And now he wished he could take it back.

Oh, he still wanted to marry her, even if it wouldn't be some legal thing where they needed someone with a license to marry them and all that, but he still wanted it. He wanted her in every way possible a man could have a woman.

"Are you mad?" Callie leaned over and whispered.

His eyes roamed her face from her soft lips to those beautiful golden eyes, over her light freckles to her slightly upturned nose. "No." He wasn't. Disappointed, yeah. But again, she hadn't exactly outright refused him. He should've known better. She'd grown up being pushed into the shadows; no way would she be comfortable being thrust into the spotlight like that. "I'm sorry," he said, pulling her hand to his lips and feathering a kiss across her knuckles. "That was stupid."

"But you do want to marry her, right?" Nova asked. Of course, they could count on the outspoken woman to break into their moment.

Without turning his eyes from Callie's face, he nodded. "Yeah. But when she's ready. And when I've pulled my head out of my ass and figured out how to ask her right."

"Awww. See? I knew there was some squishiness in you somewhere," Nova crowed.

Callie's smile spread and Micah couldn't help but mirror it. He loved when she smiled. He loved when she was happy.

He loved everything about her.

His heart practically skipped a beat as he realized he was falling hard for the woman he'd made his mate. He'd known he cared about her from the beginning, had known his wolf was obsessed. Hell, who was he kidding? He was just obsessed from the moment she tore through their yard and plowed right over their lawn chairs.

He'd known from the moment he locked eyes with her she'd end up changing his life, although he didn't know at the time how. Or how much she'd change everything about him, about the way he saw the world around him. He had no idea he could ever feel so strongly about another person after Heather died.

As the day stretched into evening, Reed lit a fire and more beers were consumed. He'd never seen Callie so relaxed. She'd even drank a few and was definitely feeling the effects as she stood and wobbled a little.

"Whoa there," he teased, throwing a hand out to steady her.

"Uh oh. Another light weight," Nova said with a chuckle. "Don't worry, Callie. I hold the title for world's biggest light weight in the Shifter class." Her smile faltered a little. "Damn, I really want a beer."

"I'm not drunk," Callie argued. "I just stood up too fast." But she'd pressed her lips into a thin line to hide the smile.

"Yeah. Just be careful. The ground likes to jump up and trip you when you, uh, stand up too fast," Nova said, not bothering to hide her grin.

"Guess we'll head out," Carter said, standing and stretching. "Let us know if you hear anything from Alan."

"I'll call you if my dad calls me first," Colton said, shoving his hat on his head and bending to press a kiss to the top of Nova's head.

Big River Pack stood and shook hands with the rest of the guys as they all said their goodnights, and Micah and Gray both growled like idiots when anyone hugged their mates. Gray had been with Nova for a while and he still acted like that, so Micah needed to cut himself a little slack, even if both Nova and Callie glared any time they showed any possessiveness.

"Night," Nova called out once Blackwater and Ravenwood drove off.

"Night," Callie called back.

Emory waved over her shoulder and trudged up her stairs. The day had gone well and they'd gotten the news they'd hoped for, but Micah feared it was far from over. By Emory's silence throughout the evening, it was obvious she felt the same way. She was still unmated and unmarked. Until the laws were completely rewritten, there would still be others who tried to con her into their group for one reason or another. Mainly to breed more Shifters into their Packs.

Finally, Micah had Callie alone. They were in her house and he couldn't help but watch her as she moved around the house, pulling a cup from the little shelf over the sink and filling it with water. After a few minutes, she turned to him, her brows pulled together.

"What?" she asked with a curious smile.

"I love you," he blurted out, unable to hold it back any longer. He thought he'd burst from the moment he'd realized how crazy he was about her until he got her home and away from everyone else. "I meant it when I said I wanted to marry you. I'm sorry I threw you under the bus like that. And I don't expect you to say yes, or even want all that, but I just wanted you to know how I felt."

Her mouth had opened into a little *o* shape and her eyes were wide. She pressed a hand to her chest.

"What?" she breathed out. Her chest rose and fell quickly as her breathing increased.

"I never thought I'd find a mate. Honestly, I didn't want to. I'm not made right, not stable. But I did find you. And I'm so in love with you. I just...you're so fucking amazing. And beautiful, inside and out." He'd told her all of his secrets. And she'd not only accepted them but had held him while he cried and told him they'd honor Heather's memory by living the life she should have. She didn't condemn him for not protecting his sister better. Didn't look at him with anything but affection.

"I love you, too," she breathed out. A smile slowly spread across his face. "You look relieved," she said.

"I am. I know you care about me and I know you feel the same pull I do. I just hoped you'd feel the same way. I still say I don't deserve you, but I promise to work every day to be the man you need."

"I need *you*," she said, closing the small gap between them. She raised her hand and cupped his cheek, letting her thumb rasp over his stubble. "It's only you, Micah. I've known from that first time I saw you there was no one else for me. Okay, maybe I didn't, but my animal did. I'm yours, Micah. You don't have to prove anything to me."

She'd said the words he'd been thinking outside. Initially, they were drawn together because of their animals. It was chemistry. But their hearts had found each other. They'd found their other half.

He placed his hand over hers, holding it against his jaw. Her touch felt so good, so right. His other hand moved up her arm, across her shoulder, and gripped the back of her neck. Instead of immediately going for her mouth, he leaned down and pressed his forehead to hers.

Holy shit. She loved him, too. She loved him despite all his flaws and inner scars.

Callie gripped his shirt in her free hand and stepped forward until their bodies were touching. When Micah looked down at her, he knew everything had changed. He knew exactly what he needed to do to make her truly happy, to give her what she needed. He knew exactly what her animal needed.

Micah dipped his head and pressed his lips to hers, the pressure bruising and erotic, all at once. He was breathing heavily, yet they hadn't done anything more than profess their feelings for each other.

He needed to feel her. All of her. He needed his hands on her, his lips on her. He needed to be buried inside her. He needed to hear her cry out his name.

∞ ∞ ∞

Callie's heart raced and her lips parted as her gasps for air became shallow. Those words were what she'd always dreamed of hearing from her true mate. She'd always dreamed he was out there, searching for her even as she called silently to him. She'd never imagined her mate would be a wolf. She'd never imagined he'd be so powerful and strong. And she could've never imagined how much she'd love him.

Now, his lips were on hers, stealing her moans as his hand made a path from her wrist to her neck where his fingers splayed over the spot where lions marked their mates. The spot tingled, as if her body knew what would happen, what was coming before the night was over.

Micah walked her backward until the back of her knees hit the cushion of her futon. He reached over her and maneuvered it until it spread out into a bed, then laid her back. Crawling over her, he held his weight on his elbows while he settled into the apex of her thighs, his hardness pressing through his jeans and rubbing her just right when he rolled his hips.

They'd made love dozens of times in the time since they'd become mated. Yet, she knew this time, this night would be the one she remembered most. He wasn't hurried or desperate, but the passion pouring from him made her feel sexy and powerful.

Slowly, he pushed her shirt up her stomach, pulling his lips from her so he could follow its path with his lips. She lifted so he could pull it over her head. He didn't wait for the tank top to hit the ground before he lowered his head and licked along the valley of her breasts, kissing each swell on his way to her throat. He nipped her jawline, the pulse point on her neck, then made his way back down, circling a nipple with his tongue before drawing it between his lips. He bit down lightly, sending little shock waves through her body. His warm, calloused hand smoothed over her stomach, down her hip where he hooked his fingers in the side of her shorts and tugged. Pulling his mouth from her breast, and earning a frustrated growl—his tongue was magic on her body—he sat back on his knees and tugged her shorts over her hips and down her legs. Lifting one foot, he kissed her ankle softly, then pressed those same soft caresses of his lips to her calf, the inside of her knee, her thigh, and then swiped his tongue through her folds. He stayed there, making love to her with his mouth as she tangled her fingers in his hair, holding him in place as she lifted her hips and writhed against him. As much as she wanted to fall apart around his tongue, she was growing inpatient and wanted him inside of her.

"Micah, please," she begged, then threw her head back when he sucked her clit between his lips. She moaned and rolled her head side to side as sparks began to build low in her belly then exploded outward, curling her toes. She almost giggled at the memory of Nova referring to her orgasm as the toe curler until another wave stole all coherent thought from her brain.

As she shuddered under his attention, Micah growled against her core, sending more sensations through her body. When he lifted, he swiped the back of his hand across his mouth and chin, and for some reason, that small movement turned her on all over again. Pushing to a sitting position, she struggled with the button on his pants and zipper, desperately needing to touch him.

"Slow down," he said with a chuckle, stilling her hands in both of his. He raised them and bent forward, kissing her knuckles. His eyes locked on her face, he shoved his jeans over his hips and Callie watched him, her tongue darting out to moisten her bottom lip at the sight of his engorged dick.

She couldn't take it anymore.

Arranging herself so she was laying on her stomach, she smiled up at him briefly as she gripped his shaft in her fist.

"What are you–"

She didn't give him a chance to finish. She licked the tip of his dick, tasting the saltiness of the drop of moisture there. He inhaled sharply. Feeling braver, she circled her lips over him and slowly took the rest of his length into her mouth, closing her eyes when his hand landed on her head.

It was an odd position to get much leverage, but she bobbed her head on him, taking as much of him as she could each time.

"Shit. Stop, Callie," he said. When she moved faster, he grunted and pulled her from him. "I love your mouth on me, but I won't last long like that." His smile was apologetic and self-deprecating and so damn adorable.

He urged her onto her back again and reached down into the pocket of his jeans. They'd finally gotten condoms after he'd come in her a few weeks back. As much as she wanted a future with him, it was too early and too dangerous of a time in their lives to risk bringing children into their world.

Callie watched with her mouth watering as he rolled the latex over his dick and laid back over her, his eyes on her face. "I love you, Callie. I really, truly do."

She smiled at him and wrapped her arms around his shoulders. He slid into her slowly, their moans matching. His movements were gentle at first, as he kissed her cheeks, the stubble scraping against her soft skin. When his lips found her mouth and his tongue dipped against hers, his thrusts became needier, like he couldn't get enough of her, couldn't get close enough to her.

And then he stopped. He stared down into her eyes and seemed to be having some kind of internal conflict. The decision made, he pulled from her, turned her, and lifted her hips into the air. This was what she'd wanted for so long. And he finally felt in control enough to take her in the way of her people. To mark her the way she needed, the way she wanted.

She held herself on her hands and knees and looked at him over her shoulder, her hair hanging in her face. He gently shoved the hair away and maintained eye contact as he pushed into her again, causing her to sway a little. This position made every sensation more intense. He was hitting places she hadn't known existed, bringing her pleasure she never could've imagined.

"Tell me," he gritted through clenched teeth. "Tell me if you need me to stop." He was holding back. His hands gripped her ass tightly and his eyes dipped between where he was entering, to her eyes, then back again.

Instead of saying a word, she pushed back against him. He grunted and stilled her with his hands on her hips. His eyes had rolled closed like it was too much or like he was struggling to keep from pounding into her.

But that was exactly what she wanted. She wanted him to lose himself in her heat. She wanted to feel his unbridled power as he plunged deep into her.

"Micah," she whispered. His lids raised and his eyes were a little bluer than when he'd closed them. She said the one thing she knew would spur him on. "Fuck me."

That did it.

Micah peeled back his lips in a primal fashion, grabbed both hips in a bruising manner, and thrust into her hard. She opened her mouth and released a surprised scream. When he no longer moved, she peered at him over her shoulder again. "Please. Please don't stop."

With a satisfied grin, he pushed into her hard and stopped. Pulled from her slow, pushed into her hard and fast. And then they built a skin slapping rhythm, each pump rocking her forward, causing her breasts to sway, her pebbled nipples to brush over the pillow below her. Every sensation was too much and not enough. She needed more. She needed to come. She needed...

Another hard shove into her and Callie was falling down a long tunnel, her vision went cloudy, and her body tightened around him. Micah released a raw, guttural growl, leaned over her back, and then there were teeth piercing the flesh just below her hairline. He didn't let go until he was twitching against her.

Finally, when they were both coming down from their highs, he released her neck, licked the blood from the teeth marks, and pulled from her. She waited for his anger over causing her to bleed again, but it didn't come. She looked at him and he was staring at his new mark, but there was something like awe and pride shining in his bright blue eyes. Both sides of Micah had marked her now. She already knew she loved both sides of him. She now belonged to them both.

Micah carried her to the bathroom, her body cradled in his arms and warm against his chest, and stood with her under the shower spray. She didn't want to wash his scent from her, but he was only washing the blood from her neck that had rolled down her back and chest. He set her on her feet long enough to dry her, then carried her back to their bed.

And it was their bed. This had started out as her house, everything inside bought specifically for her if she chose to stay. But, in just over a month, everything she was and everything she had was for him, for them. She had no idea whether he felt the same way and at the moment, she didn't care. That was how she felt. And she'd grown to worry about only what she could control. Her new Pack had taught her that her feelings weren't discounted by how someone else felt about her.

"Thank you," she said as he tucked them both under the blanket and dragged her to lay on his chest. She draped her arm over him and made lazy circles around his nipple with her pinky.

"For what?" He genuinely sounded confused.

"For giving me what I needed. What I wanted. For accepting me as your mate and as a lioness."

He hummed and pulled her closer, his chin resting on top of her head. His arms were tight around her as if he were guarding her, and his heart thrummed against her ear. For one night, everything was perfect. She had no idea what would happen tomorrow or the next day, but for that moment, she'd focus only on the beauty of their new life together. And the future she'd fought for.

Chapter Nine

Callie pulled her arms over her head as she stretched. A smile pulled the corners of her mouth up before she even opened her eyes. He'd marked her again last night, but this time, he'd marked her the way her animal needed. He'd shown her once again that he accepted her, that he loved her.

Wow. He'd actually said that he'd loved her. And she finally had the chance and courage to voice it back to him. She'd always dreamed of hearing those words and saying them to her mate, but she had no idea how good it would feel.

Rolling over, she frowned at the empty space that should've been occupied by Micah's big body. He'd pulled the blankets back over her and must've snuck out at some point. How the hell had she not heard him? Even if she'd been out to the world, her animal should've heard him tiptoeing through the house, or at least heard the front door open and close.

Sitting up, she hugged the blanket around her bare breasts and looked toward the bathroom. No light and no water running, so he'd definitely left at some point. But why?

Insecurity hit her hard. No way had he run off freaked out about last night. They were past that point. Weren't they?

"Fuck!" Gray's voice boomed through her walls.

Something was way wrong. As fast as she could, she yanked pants and a shirt on and ran outside. Gray was pacing back and forth in front of his house while Nova and Emory stood watching him from the porch.

Reed, Tristan, and Micah were there, too. As she jogged over, Micah's eyes darted to hers; they were bright blue and his lips were peeled back in a snarl.

Callie skidded to a stop a few feet away, unsure of Micah's mental state as he stared at her. A few seconds went by before he shook his head hard, his eyes widening as if he'd just realized who was standing there.

"Callie," he growled out.

"What happened?" she asked, her gaze bouncing from Micah to Gray, then to Emory and Nova. Nova had tears slowly trailing down her face.

Passing Micah, Callie stepped onto the porch and her hands reached for Nova but she pulled them back. Oh no. Had something happened to the baby?

"What? What's wrong?"

"Alan and Frank went to see Tammen," Emory said.

And all the air whooshed from her lungs at those words. This kind of anger, the tears from Nova...

"Your dad?" Had Rhett or Brent killed Alan? A fresh wave of guilt slammed into her heart.

"No. Frank. When they took the news to them, Rhett challenged him. Alan tried to talk him down, tried to explain you can't challenge a council member. But...he Shifted. And..." Emory trailed off.

"Rhett killed Frank?" Callie squeaked out past her closing throat. Rhett killed Frank. He'd killed Colton's father. Because of her.

Not true. She couldn't think of it like that. She'd already decided this whole fight was no longer just about her. It was about Emory and Nova, and all female Shifters. Rhett was the only one to blame.

"Has anyone told Colton?" Callie asked.

"Carter's the one who told me," Gray said, his nostrils flaring with each breath.

"What does this mean?" Callie asked. But no one answered. They really didn't need to. She knew exactly what it meant. Not only did Rhett not accept the new law changes, but he'd been willing to kill over it. Which meant he'd have no problem killing again.

Who would be next?

"It means that mother fucker needs to die. Slowly," Micah said, his voice deep and gravelly.

"Has anyone heard from Alan? Is he okay?" Callie asked. She wanted to comfort Micah but she was more concerned about Nova right now. In her state, she needed to keep her stress level as low as possible, and Frank's death and the very real threat to all of them wasn't helping.

"He's okay," Nova said with a sniffle. "I talked to him a few minutes ago." The fact her dad was alive and safe didn't seem to calm her. Callie wasn't sure whether it was the fear of what could've happened, the fact one of her best friend's dad was dead, or the fear of their now very unsteady future was what was causing her so much angst.

"Colton?" Callie asked, looking at Gray.

His eyes were just as blue as Micah's. All the guys looked on the verge of a Shift. "He's as to be expected. He's destroyed over it and pissed. Carter's trying to keep him from going off on his own for revenge."

Gray spoke without looking at Callie. His eyes were on his mate's face and he sounded like he was repeating something he'd been told, like he was just reading from a list. There was very little emotion short of anger in his tone. But the concern on his face, that was all for his wife.

Not sure of what to do, Callie wrapped her arms around Nova's shoulders and brought her in for a hug. Nova only hugged her back for a second before pulling away and wiping both hands under her eyes.

"I can't believe that asshole would do something like that," Nova said. She took a step to her left and sat heavily in a chair. Callie could fully believe he'd do something like that. In the back of her head, she'd feared for Alan and Frank, but figured Rhett wouldn't be that stupid. He'd just declared war on the entire Shifter council.

Emory asked if Nova needed anything then stepped down from the porch. "They're going to come after me or her," she said, pointing up at Callie. "We need to go."

"Where? Where do you think you can go that this shit won't follow?" Micah asked.

Callie wanted to argue, to add something intelligent to the conversation, but her mind had other ideas. Images of the Pride attacking others through the time she'd been with Tammen played on a loop in her brain, and to make things just a little more insanity inducing, her brain decided to slap Frank's face on a couple of the attacks. She knew Frank had died fighting, but he'd died in a painful manner.

"She might be right, Micah. We've got to find some way to keep the girls safe. Those fuckers are definitely going to be after them now. If nothing else, just to prove a fucking point," Gray said. He kept glancing up at Nova every few seconds as if trying to assure himself she was still there and safe.

"Where the fuck can we take them? Obviously, the fucking council is out now. Even if any of them still wanted to help us, they're not off-limits to Rhett and his assholes," Micah said, threading his fingers on top of his head and pushing down. Callie didn't say anything out loud, but she was so proud of how well he was holding it together considering how messed up everything was.

Her eyes bouncing back and forth, Callie searched her mind for a solution, but just like the guys, she was coming up with nothing. The council was no safer than they were. If they took in the women to protect them, Rhett would attack. And the members were too old to take on that many lions and probably wolves. She had zero doubts Rhett would call in Anson and Deathport. They'd both benefit if they were able to annihilate the entire council. They'd find enough evil assholes like them and try to make their own rules. And female Shifters would once again be at the bottom of the pile.

"We could make a stand," Tristan said.

Everyone's heads whipped to him, their eyes wide. Quiet Tristan stood there with bright blue eyes as his anger riled his animal up.

"What?" Reed asked. "You don't talk and now you just throw out there that we should go up against the lions when you know full fucking well how outnumbered we are?"

Tristan shrugged, but his eyes went to Emory. There were so many emotions there; anger, fear, concern, loyalty. He'd do whatever Emory wanted, whatever she asked of him.

Gray stared at Tristan, glanced back at Nova, then dropped his head with a huff. "Fuck. No matter what we do, we're fucked."

"She's the only one we really need to worry about," Callie said, pointing at Nova. "Emory and I can fight."

"And you can be fucking taken, too," Micah said. "I'm not letting that happen."

Callie turned on Micah, her brows pulled low. "Listen, Micah. It looks like our choices are down to two: we fight and pray that we come out of this okay, or we run...and still pray that we come out of this okay. Do you really think Rhett's going to let either of us disappear after all of this? He murdered a high-ranking council member. Do you really think he'll just forget about me? About Emory? I'm tired of being afraid. I'm tired of being treated as nothing. I'm tired of *feeling* like nothing."

Emory took a step closer. She might not like her choices, but she agreed with Tristan. It was time for them to stand their ground, to fight for what they believed in.

"It's time for a fucking revolution," Callie said, almost wincing at her words. Any time she muttered the f word, it felt foreign in her mouth. But she had to get her point across. And by the way the guys' mouths were hanging open, she'd achieved just that.

"We'll need Blackwater. *And* Ravenwood," Reed said, dragging a hand down his face.

"We can't ask them—" Gray started, but Nova interrupted him.

"It was their decision, Gray. They already offered. They're our friends. They have sisters, moms, aunts...this is just as much about them as us. And I'm sure Colton would love a chance to avenge his dad," Nova said, standing and leaning forward with her hands gripping the railing of the porch.

"We've still got to find a way to keep you safe," Emory said to Nova.

Callie chewed on the inside of her cheek. It wasn't a matter of *if* Tammen would come for her but *when*. And they knew as well as she did her Pack wouldn't stand by and let that happen. No way would Micah let that happen. They had to keep Nova safe, no matter what else happened. No matter if she was taken or killed, or the lions got their hands on Emory, they had to keep Nova and little Wolfgang safe and away from the fight.

"Alan," Callie blurted out. "We could take her to him and leave her there."

"No. I don't want her out of my sight. And they took out Frank with Alan there. He got hurt. He's not fully healed yet."

"But we don't know when they'll come," Callie said.

"And until we know anything, I'm not taking a fucking chance with my mate or child."

"Would Colton or one of the other guys stick around here for a while?" Reed asked.

"I'm not asking Colton for anything right now," Gray said, his voice quiet, his eyes unfocused as he stared off into the trees.

Grief for Colton slammed into Callie again. He'd lost his father. Because he was fighting for Callie, for Emory, for all women. Even though he'd fought for his life, even though he'd died because of something so honorable, it didn't lessen the amount of guilt she'd probably carry for the rest of her life over Frank's death. She had to find a way to honor him, just as she'd said she'd honor Heather.

So many lives lost because of the Shifters who believed they could take whatever they wanted, because they felt they had the right to treat another living being as nothing. More lives might be lost, but it was worth the sacrifice, even if hers was one of those lives.

She looked around at her Pack; she just prayed none of these people would be a sacrifice. She needed them to go on; keep Micah safe and help him find happiness again if something happened to her. She needed them to keep fighting for women. Fighting for freedom. She needed them to carry on her memory.

∞ ∞ ∞

Micah couldn't stand to be more than two feet away from Callie since they'd gotten the news about Frank. The Pack was solemn, quiet. They'd all retreated into their own houses. He wanted to Shift, wanted to give his animal his body and run, release some of the pent-up anger and energy, but he didn't want to leave Callie's side. He couldn't stand the thought of not being able to see her, to touch her. And she hadn't wanted to run with him.

She sat on her folded-up futon with her knees pulled up to her chin, her arms wrapped around her shins as she stared at the far wall.

"I'm scared," she admitted just above a whisper.

He scooted closer until he could wrap his arm around her shoulders and hug her into his side. She rested her head against his chest and he heard a soft sniffle that broke his fucking heart. He hated Tammen. He hated Rhett. He wanted them all dead.

But above the hate and anger was fear, raw, unadulterated fear. He feared for his mate, he feared for Emory, and he feared for Nova. Images of Heather's lifeless body floated through his head and he lifted his free hand to push a fist against his forehead. Those weren't images he needed right now. He needed to think positively or some shit. He had to think like Nova and pretend everything would just work itself out somehow.

"I'll protect you," Micah said.

"I know you will. But I'm just as scared for you." She leaned her knees so they were pressed against him and settled one hand on his chest. "I need you to promise me something."

"Don't even fucking say it, Callie," Micah said, his body going tense. He knew without her uttering a single word what she was going to ask him.

"Micah—"

"Let me guess: promise me you'll go on if something happens to me, Micah," he said, raising his voice an octave to imitate her. "Promise me that no matter what happens you'll find happiness again. How did I do?"

Instead of getting pissed or pushing away from him, Callie surprised him and snorted. "Okay. Now that you said it out loud, it sounds silly."

"Could you just go on and find another mate if something happened to me?" he said.

She did push away this time and look up into his face. "You proved your point."

Oh, he wanted to push it further, but the look on her face stopped him before he opened his mouth. The pain from just the thought of a life without Micah was there in her eyes. He didn't want to be the cause of any more.

So, he pulled her back to his chest and rested his chin on top of her head. "Would it make you feel better if I said it'll be okay?"

"No. But say it anyway," she said, snuggling closer to him. Her thin arm wedged itself behind his back and her other arm draped over chest.

He kissed the top of her head. "It'll be okay," he whispered against her hair. "You have to promise me something."

She jerked her head up. "Didn't we already go through all this?" Her blonde brows created a little crease.

He chuckled once. "I want you to promise you'll fight as hard as you've ever fought. Let your lioness loose, let her go fucking crazy. Use those claws like you did on my wolf. Kill any fucker who tries to touch you, Callie. Don't worry about what I'm doing or anyone else. Focus on keeping yourself alive."

She nodded her head against his chest, but he knew what was going through that pretty head. She was thinking about Emory, about Nova, about her Pack. She was thinking about ways to keep everyone safe at the same time.

"Callie, this isn't the first time this Pack has had to fight. We'll be fine. Keep yourself safe. I need to know you'll fight so I can focus on everything else."

Sucking in a deep breath, Callie nodded again. "Okay. Yeah. I promise," she said, but her tone was reluctant.

He hugged her tight and just breathed her in, memorizing everything about her, her scent, the way her breath warmed his chest through his shirt, the way her arms were tight around his waist. They had no idea how long they had before Tammen tried to come for her. They had no idea if they'd all survive. All he knew was he'd spend his last breath keeping her safe.

"I love you, Callie," he whispered.

"I love you, too."

Micah fell asleep with Callie in his arms. When he opened his eyes, the moon cast a silver glow on the walls.

His arms were empty and Callie wasn't lying beside him on the couch. A soft sound on the front porch had him on his feet and rushing to the door. It wasn't just her soft voice he could hear; there was a male out there and he caught the scent before he was even outside.

Micah's hand was around Eli's throat and lifting him against the side of the house the second the door was ripped open.

"What the fuck are you doing here?" Micah bellowed in Eli's face.

Callie's hands were on Micah's forearms, yanking and trying to pry him from Eli. "Micah, stop. Listen."

"Back the fuck up, Callie," Micah said as his animal tried to force its way from his skin. He'd never fought so hard for restraint as he had since Callie had come into his life. He wanted to be a better man for her, be someone who deserved her.

But finding a member of the Tammen Pride with his mate on her front porch in the middle of the night was way more than he could handle.

"Fuck. Callie, please," he begged as his teeth grew in his mouth.

"Gray!" Callie screamed as loud as she could.

One by one, doors opened and feet thundered across the hard ground.

"What the fuck is this?" Gray growled out.

Micah didn't pull his eyes from Eli's face, but he could sense the rest of his Pack nearby.

"Eli came to warn us. Micah, please stop. Let him go." Callie was pulling at his arms again.

"Micah, let him go. He can't talk if he can't breathe," Gray said, stepping beside Micah.

"Fuck him. He doesn't need to say shit."

He was trembling with the strength to keep from Shifting while Callie was touching him. His animal might know their mate, but he didn't trust him right now with the enemy so fucking close.

"Please, listen to me, Micah. He's here to help," Callie begged. She let go of his wrists and took a step back. Smart mate.

"Help how?" Gray asked. He'd taken another step closer and placed a hand on Micah's shoulder.

"He was trying to warn me," Callie said, panic lacing her words.

"Let him go," Gray said, his voice taking on that powerful sound as he shoved Micah away.

Micah released his grip and let Eli fall hard onto the porch. He gasped and wheezed as he rubbed at the red marks on his throat.

"What the fuck, man," Eli said as he climbed to his feet. His eyes had bled to gold. Good. If his lion wanted a fucking fight, Micah was ready.

Hands were on him again, but this time they were bigger and stronger. Reed and Tristan pulled him away and down the steps onto the patch of dry grass in front of Callie's house.

"Get him away from her!" he bellowed. Callie stood just a few feet from Eli, and his animal was trying to scratch and tear his way through Micah's skin.

"Micah, I'm fine," she said, but climbed down the stairs to stand with him. "Just stop and listen, please."

"Fuck you. I'm gone," Eli said, still rubbing his throat.

Eli stomped down the steps and toward a car parked a couple yards from their trucks. They'd all thought there was no way anyone could ever sneak up on them, yet there Eli was. He'd driven right onto their property, walked right past everyone's house, and somehow got Callie's attention from inside the house.

"Why the fuck was no one patrolling the property?" Micah demanded, his eyes never leaving Eli as he continued to his Mustang.

"Eli, wait," Callie called out and tried to run to him.

Micah wrapped a hand around her bicep and pulled her to a stop. "What are you doing? Did you not think his being here could be a fucking trap?"

"Would you all chill out and listen to what he has to say? Eli, come back. No one's going to touch you. I promise."

"Don't promise anything. Because if he even looks at you wrong, I'll kill the fucker," Micah said.

"Eli, why are you here?" Gray yelled across the few yards separating the lion from the Pack.

Micah tipped his head to each side, cracking his neck, and leveled his gaze on Eli as he turned and slowly made his way back, his eyes never leaving Micah. He was ready for an attack. But so was Micah.

"Rhett's coming," he said.

Micah's already racing heart tripped and his eyes darted around the surrounding dark woods. "When?" he growled out. It was no longer his voice. He still had control over his body but his wolf was right there with him, watching, waiting, ready to kill to protect his mate.

"I don't know. Soon. He's got the entire Pride fucked up," Eli said, taking a few steps closer.

"Fucked up, how?" Reed asked. He stood there naked, his arms crossed over his chest. Micah looked around and realized the only people wearing any clothing besides Eli were the girls.

Good. Micah didn't want this asshole to see his mate's body. And he knew Gray felt the same way. Nova stood on the porch, not daring to come closer. Again, good. With her away from what could be a shit load of action if Eli made a move or this turned into some kind of trap allowed the rest of the Pack to focus on the looming threat.

"Half of them are freaking out over...what he did to the council member."

"His name was Frank," Gray said, his posture relaxed but his muscles were tense. Micah knew Gray was just as on edge.

"They don't want this, Gray. They don't want a fight. They want to live a normal life." Eli took a few more steps closer and Micah couldn't take much more.

He walked forward, blocking Eli's path to Callie. "Don't take another fucking step," he said low.

Eli glanced over Micah's shoulder then back at Micah. "We have females in the Pride. Cubs. I'm doing what I can to protect them, but Rhett is already trying to force them to fight beside him."

"Oh, and you suddenly care about the females?" Reed said. He moved until he was standing beside Micah, their shoulders almost touching.

"I've always cared. Not of all us think the same way Rhett does, asshole," Eli said to Reed. "I'm trying to help you. To help the women in my Pride."

"You said Rhett was coming. You still haven't said any more than *soon*," Gray said. He was standing next to Reed now, the three men shoulder to shoulder, the anger rolling off them in waves. It did nothing to calm Micah's animal. He needed to touch Callie but didn't want her any closer than she was.

"That's all I know. He's coming, and he's talking to Anson about joining him. They want to take over the area. They don't like the new law changes," Eli said, pushing a hand through his auburn hair roughly. "If this comes to battle...*when* this comes to a battle, there will be females fighting. Not all of them want to be involved. But Rhett isn't giving them much choice. All I'm asking is you not kill them. Let them return to their cubs."

"Let them return to slavery?" Emory called from behind the wall of men.

"Listen," Eli said, stepping to the side to see Emory better.

Tristan stepped closer to Emory while the other men tensed and growled.

Eli looked each person in the eye before looking back at Emory. "Not all lions want that shit. You don't owe me shit—"

"Got that right," Reed said.

"But you have to trust me. There are a lot of us who don't live that way. I've never had a mate in my life. I don't want someone who doesn't want me. There's been talk since Frank's death, talk about overthrowing Rhett, about taking over the Pride."

"And which of you lovely assholes would become Alpha?" Reed asked.

Eli shrugged. "Don't know and don't care, as long as it's not Rhett. Take him out and things can change."

"Unless Brent takes over," Callie said.

Micah looked over his shoulder at his mate. She'd taken a few steps closer but she was still far enough away to keep his animal at bay.

"I hate that fucker, but even he's better than Rhett."

"What about you?" Emory asked.

Eli raised his eyes to look at Emory. "What about me?"

"Why don't you challenge him and take over?"

Eli dropped his head, snorted, and shook his head with a wry smile. "I'm not a fucking Alpha. I just want to live my life, find a mate someday, one who wants me back, and die old and happy. As long as

Rhett is on this warpath, we're all fucked. I've gotta go. Call your friends. You're going to need them."

He turned his back and took long strides back to his Mustang.

"Why would we need our friends?" Nova called from the front porch.

Gray and Micah both quickly made their way to stand directly in front of where she leaned against the railing.

Eli stopped with his door open, his hand on the window. "If Anson joins Rhett, you won't have a fucking chance. Find somewhere to hide her. She won't be any safer," Eli said, pointing at Nova.

With Gray growling nonstop, Eli dropped into his Mustang, turned it over, and rolled out of their property, leaving that last ominous warning hanging in the air over them like a fucking guillotine.

∞ ∞ ∞

Callie stood with her arms wrapped around her middle, watching the dust from Eli's tires as he left the Pack territory. When he'd tapped on the window of her little door, she'd thought for sure it was all over. Tammen had successfully snuck up on Big River, had killed all her friends, and now they would drag her back to Pride territory.

But it had only been Eli. Just him. He'd stood there with his hands in the air, like he was surrendering to the police. With a glance at Micah and going against her better judgment, she'd joined Eli on the porch. She'd figured if they were there for her, Micah would be safe if she went without a fight. She needed him safe, she needed him still alive.

There were no other Pride members, no lions stalking around outside with bloody mouths. It had been just Eli. She'd only been out there with him for maybe two minutes when Micah had come rushing through the door and slammed him against the wall by his throat.

And now, they all stood there, unsure of what to do with his news.

"What the fuck did he mean Nova won't be any safer? She's pregnant with a wolf. She's fucking mated," Reed said, finally turning his back on Eli's retreating car when the taillights disappeared around the corner.

"What do lions do in the wild when a male takes over the Pride?" Callie said, hugging herself tighter.

She glanced up at Nova. She mimicked Callie's body language, hugging the swell of her stomach, protecting her unborn baby the best she could.

"That sick fuck," Micah said then spit in the dirt.

He hadn't Shifted and killed Eli. That was huge for him, huge for his animal. Again, she was proud of him but kept her mouth shut. Now was the time for logistics.

Eli's warning made bile rise in Callie's throat. What did lions do in the wild? They killed the young of their predecessor. They made sure only their bloodline existed. And, apparently, Rhett was intent on taking a cue from their pure blood ancestors.

"Call Alan," Gray said, pointing at Nova. "Get him up to date, ask for suggestions. I'll call Carter. Reed, call Aron. I'm not taking any chances that Eli wasn't some form of fucked up decoy, some way of getting us all out here." He looked around at the Pack, his eyes bright in the moonlight. "Fuck!" he yelled at the night sky, his head tipped back. Gray turned and stared at his mate, his eyes still bright but now there was a shimmer to them as he fought back tears. Tears of anger or tears of fear, Callie didn't know. But she didn't bother holding her own back.

She opened her mouth to tell them all she'd just surrender, return to the Pride, and take whatever punishment they doled out. Yeah, she knew it would be bad, had no doubt Brent would make an example of her. But these people would be safe.

And then she looked at Emory, who looked absolutely terrified. Her eyes were wide and her lips were parted as she gasped in breaths of air. Even if Callie went back to the Pride, Emory would never be safe. And, apparently, neither would Nova or any other female-born Shifter.

She had to remember this was no longer about her; they were fighting for the future of hundreds of thousands of Shifters, females who were born with no choice about their own lives, little girls who were forced into pairings with cruel men, teenagers who were sold to Prides and Packs by their own fathers.

Long after Callie was gone, after Emory and Nova and even little Wolfgang were gone, there would still be Shifters on this planet. This was a fight for her species and her gender.

So, they'd fight. They'd fight for their lives, they'd fight for Callie's and Emory's freedom, and they'd fight for female Shifters around the world.

Chapter Ten

It had been a week since Eli's abrupt appearance. The Blackwater Clan stuck around a lot. Colton only came by once and he about broke Callie's heart. His eyes were puffy from all the tears he'd no doubt shed over his father's death. They'd had a small ceremony to tell him goodbye and it had been filled with so much tension. There had been guards set around the property. Shifters from outside Clans had come from all over Missouri to pay their respects and make sure Frank's funeral wasn't interrupted by Rhett or any of his asshole enforcers.

Carter was over again. He sat on the steps of Gray's house, his elbows on his knees, his phone to his ear.

"Who's he talking to now?" Callie asked Emory.

Everyone had pretty much put their lives on hold. Emory had called in to work sick indefinitely. There was a pretty good chance she wouldn't have a job when this was all over. Carter had put all their construction jobs on hold until further notice, citing issues with their equipment. As much as that sucked, they'd finally gotten some rain, so they would've been off during that time anyway.

But they'd eventually have to go back to work, back to their jobs, back to their normal lives.

"Aron. Carter's trying to find a way to keep Nova safe. She could have that baby within a few weeks. Even if she could Shift after she gives birth, she'll need to stay with Wolfgang, keep the lions away from him."

The thought of Rhett killing Nova's baby made Callie's stomach turn. Only a sick bastard could hurt a child. And Rhett was exactly that kind of sick bastard. Anything to gain power, anything to gain control, anything to keep his little harem intact.

Voices raised inside of Gray and Nova's house, then the front door swung in and Nova waddled out, pushing past Carter and dropping into one of the lawn chairs arranged in a circle.

"It's not a good idea," Gray said, hurrying to kneel in front of his mate.

"Whatever. That's what I want. It might be the last one we have before..." She waved her hand around her belly. "Everything changes. How could it be a bad thing to have everyone we love over? It's not like I said to invite the lions."

Emory and Callie shuffled over to Nova and sat on each side of her. "Cookout?" Emory asked, forcing a smile.

"Why not? Let's get everyone together, cook some cow, have some beers...or iced tea," she said with a roll of her eyes. "How many more will we have? How many more opportunities will we have to get everyone together?"

She didn't need to say the words, but Callie knew exactly what she was thinking: How many more opportunities would there be to get everyone still alive together? Because there was a high probability quite a few of them would die when Rhett decided to attack.

"I think we should do it. Hey, we'll have everyone here. It'll be the safest this Pack will ever be," Callie said. What she'd wanted to say was it was the safest she, Emory, and Nova would ever be.

Gray glanced at Callie then back at his mate. He studied her, his eyes bouncing between hers, then dropped his head with a sigh. "I don't think drinking is a great idea," he muttered. He raised his head and looked at Nova again. "Fine. I'll send out the text."

"Yay!" Nova cheered, clapping her hands, but the usual lightness about her, the usual easy manner was gone. Her excitement was forced.

Gray took a few steps away and pulled his phone from his back pocket. Carter ended the call and stood, so Gray made his way over to him and told him Nova's plans.

"You doing okay?" Callie asked, leaning her elbow on the armrest.

"I've been having contractions all day," she said, wrinkling her nose. "I looked it up. It's normal. It's still too early. And they're not bad, but I think little Wolfy is coming sooner than we thought."

That sent excitement and dread coursing through Callie. "Does Gray know?"

She shook her head slowly. "Nope. And not telling him until after everyone's gone. This might be my last childless get together and I plan to enjoy every second of it. So, if either of you hussies blab, I'll make you change poopy diapers until my kid turns two."

Emory snorted. Callie smiled. Then Emory chuckled. All three women threw their heads back and laughed. It was the first outburst of genuine laughter anyone had had since Eli had shown up. Hell, it might've been even longer than that.

Micah's front door opened and closed and he stood on his porch, staring at her. The mark on the back of her neck tingled from his one gaze. He'd gone back to his place early that morning to shower and change clothes, but Callie knew he just needed some time alone, some time to think. They'd spent every night since she'd been there together and in her place. He only left long enough to grab more clothes a few times a week. So the fact he wanted to get ready away from her, the fact he'd left her still in bed, kissing her on the cheek before he left, told her there was way more going on in his head than he was willing to say.

Climbing down the steps, Micah made his way to her and bent over the back of the chair to press his mouth to hers. He didn't push for more, didn't slide his tongue along her lips. Just held his kiss to her before pulling back and taking a chair beside hers.

"Cookout?" he asked, taking his eyes from hers and turning them on Nova.

If he'd heard them discuss that, what were the chances he'd heard Nova's declaration about her contractions?

"Yeah. Want to get at least one more in before I'm lugging around a crying baby," Nova said, leaning her head back and closing her eyes.

It was such a beautiful day—so sunny and the temperature was perfect for lazing around and doing nothing. One by one, the rest of the Pack joined them, including Carter.

"Everyone will be here in about an hour. Colton's picking up the food and beer," Carter said, taking a seat beside Gray.

"Colton's coming?" Nova said, lifting her head and smiling.

"Yeah," Carter said, rubbing his hand over his hair. He looked exhausted and stressed. Then again, so did all of the Big River Pack.

Less than an hour later, trucks came pulling up carrying the men from the Blackwater Clan and the Ravenwood Pride.

One by one, they climbed from their cabs and carried over arms full of bags while Colton lugged over their blue cooler and set it just outside the circle of chairs. He kissed Nova on the head and nodded at Callie. She couldn't see his eyes behind his sunglasses, but she knew his eyes were probably swollen with emotion. His usual black cowboy hat was missing and his dark blond hair stood up as if he'd been running his fingers through it constantly.

Even as he sat in a chair a few down from Callie, his shoulders looked rolled forward as if he were carrying a heavy weight. He looked exhausted. No; he looked defeated.

"How you doing, Colton?" Nova asked. He shrugged. "Anything we can do?"

Colton pulled his sunglasses off and scrubbed his eyes with both hands. When he dropped them, he looked directly at Callie for a few moments before answering. She feared his answer, feared he did, indeed, blame her for what happened to his dad. A wicked smile curved the corners of his lips up and he turned his eyes to Nova. "I get to be the one to kill Rhett." That was all he said. Just those eight words, but they'd felt like he'd screamed them.

"He's all yours," Gray said.

"I don't know. Pretty sure that fucker's mine," Micah said, standing and pulling two beers from the cooler.

"You can have Brent. Rhett's mine. Mine. No one takes him out but me," Colton said, looking each person in the eye.

Each of them nodded. Was this all really going to happen? Were they really going to have to go up against the entire damn Pride?

Yeah. It was going to happen. Callie knew that even if Tammen didn't come for her and her Pack, Blackwater, or at least Colton, would be hunting down the Alpha fairly soon. At least Carter was making sure Colton grieved before going off half-cocked.

Unlike every other get together they'd had since Callie had joined the Pack, this particular one was heavy and solemn. They still joked and played, but the conversation continuously went to plans, how they were going to be on the offensive end of this rather than playing defense. Callie had never really been in a fight other than defending herself, but this all seemed like a lot.

But could they ever really be overly prepared?

Callie glanced around the circle at everyone sitting there, at her friends who'd joined them on their territory, at her new family sitting nearby, at Nova sitting beside her. Nova's arm lifted quickly and stroked her belly; Callie knew she was probably having another contraction but didn't want to say anything and cause stress. As she stared at Nova's round belly and thought about the child getting ready to join the world, she realized they might never be truly prepared for what was coming.

"You okay?" Gray whispered to his mate, leaning over to press a kiss to her shoulder.

Nova winced, her brows pulling together tightly. Uh oh. "Actually...I think I'm in labor," she admitted.

"What?!" every single person around the fire barked out.

Nova jumped then frowned. "Well, good thing my water didn't break yet because that probably would've scared the kid right out of me."

"How long?" Gray asked, his tone calm but Callie could see it in his eyes, in the tight knit of his brows.

"About an hour...ish. It was okay at first. I was having small contractions. But they're getting stronger. And closer together."

"Holy shit," Reed said. And then his smile widened. "I'm going to be an uncle tonight."

"That's not true. She could be in labor for a while," Emory said.

"If you want to live, I suggest never saying that to me again," Nova said, blowing a long breath of air out through puckered lips.

"What do we do?" Callie asked as she stood then sat again. She sat wringing her hands, watching Nova with wide eyes. Maybe she should've just risked pissing Nova off and told Gray earlier what was going on.

"Call Alan. Tell him to get a midwife," Carter said, standing and moving closer to Nova. "What can I get you, Nova?"

She rolled her eyes up to him as another contraction hit. This time, instead of just breathing through it, a low, keening sound escaped her lips. "Revenge on every jackass who ever put a woman through this," Nova said.

Reed barked out a laugh. "That right there is why I never want a mate," he said with a shake of his head.

∞ ∞ ∞

Callie waited outside with everyone else as Gray stood inside, leaned against the door as the Shifter mid-wife checked over Nova and the baby. They'd had a girl; Nova had been right. And Reed was not happy.

"Another girl in the Pack?" he whined.

"Oh, come on. Now we're finally even," Emory said, a wide smile on her face as she, just like everyone else, stared at the windows and waited.

The moment they'd heard Nova's last scream followed by an infant wail was by far the happiest and most belly turning moment of any of their lives. Callie might have only been with this group for a short time, but she knew everything would be different from here out. Everything would revolve around that little girl in those four walls.

"Dude, you don't think she's going to name her Wolfgang-ette, do you?" Reed asked, shifting his weight to try to see through the bigger window in front.

Micah snorted and shook his head, while a few others groaned. Honestly, one never knew what Nova would do. She was always full of surprises and kept them all on their toes.

Gray moved away from the door, then it opened and Alan stepped outside, a smile wide on his face. He looked around at the group waiting anxiously to get a glimpse of the baby. "I'm a grandpa!" he yelled, raising his fists in the area triumphantly.

They cheered with him, then abruptly shut up when Gray peeked his head out with a scowl and slashed his hand through the air.

"Sorry," Reed whispered before Gray could close the door.

"I'm dying. I need to hold that baby," Emory said, clasping her hands in front of her and practically dancing in place.

"You think she'll be more like Gray or Nova?" Colton asked.

Micah smiled, just a quirk of his lips. "I'm sure Nova's genes dominated and we'll have another sassy little girl running around."

Callie smiled up at her mate and stepped into his side. It was probably silly with everything on their laps at the moment, but she allowed herself to pretend the excited and proud look on Micah's face was for their own child. She tried to imagine what kind of father he'd be, how he'd teach their child to Shift, how he'd teach them to hunt, how he'd rock them in his strong arms when they cried.

"You look happy," Micah whispered into her ear, bending to press a kiss at the sensitive spot there.

Callie smiled wider and let him nuzzle into her neck. "I am."

Micah pulled away and looked into her eyes, opened his mouth, but shut it and turned when the front door to Gray's opened again.

Gray's eyes were on the bundle in his arms as he stepped onto the porch, a wistful smile on his face. Nova was still inside, but she'd need time to rest after giving birth with zero meds to help with the pain.

When Gray looked up at the group of people, he moved his arms a little so everyone could see the baby's face. "I have a daughter," he said, his voice soft and full of so much mushiness Callie couldn't hold back the girly *aww*.

"Please tell me you didn't name her Wolfgang-ette," Reed said, breaking the little spell they were all in as they stared at the tiny, pink little girl swaddled in a purple and blue blanket.

Gray smiled wider and looked at Reed. "Her name is Rieka. It means a woman who has the power of the wolf," he said, looking back down at his daughter.

"That's so beautiful," Emory said, pushing forward and climbing the stairs so she could get a better look. She pushed the corner of the blanket down a little more so she could see all of Rieka's face, see her tiny hands balled into fists.

"Way better than Wolfgang," Reed muttered, but it sounded distracted as he, too, moved closer to see little Rieka.

No one spoke. They all just stared at the little miracle who'd finally joined their lives, their Pack. Even the Blackwater and Ravenwood guys couldn't seem to get close enough as they stared down at the baby.

"I can't wait to spoil her," Emory said.

"I can't wait to hold her," Callie admitted.

But not yet. As much as she wanted to reach her arms out and feel the weight and warmth from the girl, she'd wait until Gray and Nova got their fill. But after that…she had a feeling Rieka wouldn't be put down for a long time.

Chapter Eleven

Micah stood on the front porch and watched the sun rise. Nova had given birth to little Rieka three days ago, and he hadn't been able to sleep more than an hour or two at a time since. Fear that the fucking Tammen Pride would come for them when they were so vulnerable kept his animal too close to the surface. He'd even feared making love to his mate for fear of losing it with her.

Of course, that didn't exactly bode well with Callie. She'd tried to seduce him, had reminded him she was a Shifter, just like him, and could take whatever he gave, but that didn't put him at ease. Just because she'd heal didn't mean he wanted to cause her any pain. It had taken him weeks to get over the fact he'd drawn blood from her three times.

Stirring inside had Micah turning and looking over his shoulder. Callie was sitting up and frowning at him.

"What are you doing?" she asked, her voice only slightly muffled through the door.

"Couldn't sleep," he answered, keeping his voice low so he wouldn't wake anyone else. Everyone needed their sleep, especially the new parents.

Alan had elected to stay within their territory, sleeping on Reed's floor, although he'd tried to get the elder to sleep on the couch. Alan wanted to be near his daughter and new granddaughter. Or at least that's what he'd said. Micah couldn't help but wonder if the same fears that plagued him every night weren't running through Alan's head.

What really freaked Micah out was they'd all eventually have to return to work. The ground was drying after the last rain, so they'd have to return to the work site to finish the new subdivision going up. But he really didn't want to stray too far from home. The site was at least twenty minutes away; that was twenty minutes Nova, Rieka, Callie, and Emory would be unprotected while the Pack hurried home.

"Come back to bed," Callie said, pulling the blanket back.

With a heavy sigh, he turned the knob and pushed the door open. He knew he wouldn't sleep, but holding Callie in his arms when she was all warm and naked like she was sounded like the kind of perfection he wanted.

Shucking his jeans, he climbed under the blanket, wrapped his arms around her, and pulled her until her upper body was lying draped across his chest. He kissed the top of her hair and held her as her breathing became even again. She was so soft and warm. Her leg was resting between his thighs where the top of her knee grazed his junk, and her arm was wrapped around his waist.

Bliss.

He laid still while she slept for another hour. And then, finally, she began to rouse on her own. As much as he loved holding her, his arm and shoulder had gone to sleep a while ago and now pins and needles stabbed at him as the blood rushed back to his extremities.

Callie rolled onto her back and stretched her arms and legs, her toes pointed. "Good morning," she said around a yawn. Rolling onto her side, she folded her hands under her cheek and looked at him. "Did you get anymore sleep?"

He shook his head. "No."

"What's going on in there?" she asked, brushing her fingertips across his forehead.

He rolled onto his side to look at her fully. "Rieka," he said.

She nodded, her cheek brushing against the pillow. "You're worried Tammen will come and she'll be in danger." He nodded. "We'll keep her safe. Alan's here, too. And Blackwater and—"

"It's not enough. None of it is nearly enough. Even with the Clan and other Pride, we're still going to be outnumbered. Our attentions will be torn trying to keep all four of you girls safe."

"Emory and I can fight." He opened his mouth to argue, but she pressed her fingertips against his lips. "Stop. I get it. I know what you're going to say, but we can fight. I might not be as cool as you guys and have fought a million times before, but my lion knows her Pack and will tear into anyone who comes close to her mate. When they come, just focus on staying safe and I'll keep the baby and Nova safe. I won't let anyone hurt Rieka."

"She's not the only one I'm worried about," he admitted, and felt a little shitty for not solely worrying about the infant a few doors down.

"I know. Honestly, I'm kind of scared. Don't get all feral coyote on me here," she said, and he winced at her mention of his mixed animal. She smiled to soften the comment. "I'd rather die fighting for what I believe in and for who I love than hide like some coward while you guys risk yourselves. Not happening."

Micah leaned forward until their foreheads were touching. He grabbed both of her hands and pulled them from under her cheek and held them in his. "I love you," he breathed out.

He did. So fucking much. He was so fucking terrified of what could happen when Tammen came, and he had no doubt they were plotting something while the Big River Pack walked a razor line of anxiety. But even where there was fear in his heart, there was so much pride in his woman, in her strength and bravery. She'd been a little broken when she'd showed up on their doorstep, and now, she was ready to take on the world to keep her people safe.

"I love you, too," she said, bringing his hands to her chest and squeezing them. "I'm hungry," she said after a few minutes of them just holding each other like that.

Micah chuckled and pulled back. He pressed his lips to her forehead, then climbed from the bed and made his way into the kitchen naked. "You want a real breakfast or something light?" he asked.

She was sitting up, her weight on her elbows, watching him. Her eyes were hooded and she was checking him out head to toe. "I'm looking at what I want for breakfast," she said, her voice full of lust.

They did eventually eat, but not until after they'd made love and he'd made her moan out his name...twice.

Callie was showering as Micah leaned against the sink, brushing his teeth. Such a domesticated moment, like they'd lived this way for twenty years. Like an old married couple. And the idea of marriage once again came to him. This time, though, he didn't blurt it out like an idiot. He was definitely going to ask her again, definitely wanted to make her his wife, but when he asked next time, he'd do it the right way. He'd get her a ring that was perfect for her and find a way to ask her that would make her happy. And then they'd have whatever kind of wedding she wanted, whether it was some big, frilly deal in a church somewhere, or something like Nova and Gray had with just their closest friends on the front lawn.

When she stepped out with a towel wrapped around her middle, water droplets dripping from the ends of her blonde hair to run down her shoulder and chest, Micah was tempted to rip the fabric away and take her again. But they had things to do today, whether he liked it or not.

"We have to go to work today. But not for long," he told her as she dried her hair with another towel.

"Okay," she said, leaning to the side as she squeezed at her hair.

"I don't want to," he admitted.

Tossing the towel she'd used on her hair on the rack, Callie crossed her arms and leaned her butt against the sink. "We'll be fine. Even if you guys are a little further away, Blackwater can get here in ten."

"I still don't like it. I'm supposed to protect you," he said, pushing a clump of damp hair behind her ear.

"And I'm supposed to protect you," she said, raising one brow. "If I think anything seems off at all, I'll call you immediately. Just get to work, get done, and come home. I'll make you dinner tonight," she said, standing on her tiptoes to press a kiss to his lips.

He wrapped his arms around her and pulled her up his body, causing the towel to shift a little. When the knot at her side came undone and the towel fluttered to the ground, Callie smiled against his lips. "You did that on purpose," she said against his mouth.

With a shrug, he lowered her back to her feet and just drank in the sight of his naked mate. "Maybe."

A horn blared from outside and Micah groaned. He'd thought he'd have at least a few more minutes with his mate, but they had to make money. "I've got to go. I'll have my phone on me all day."

"I'm sure Gray's will be attached to his ear. We'll be fine. Emory and I will probably just hang out with Nova all day."

"You mean you'll hang out with Rieka all day," he teased with a swat on her bare ass. The sharp sound made his dick twitch and he inwardly cursed adult responsibilities. "When all this is over, when there's no more assholes trying to steal you away or threatening our

Pack, when it's just us building our lives, I'm going to marry you," he said, destroying all those plans he'd made in his head of how he was going to propose properly. "And then, I'm going to take you somewhere private and worship your body nonstop for at least a week."

"Sounds good to me," she said, her voice suddenly breathless.

"You'll marry me?"

"Are you officially asking this time?" she asked, scooping the towel from the ground and covering herself. He'd much rather she stayed naked.

"For the record, the first two times were official. I just didn't do it right." The horn honked again, this time longer. If that wasn't Gray honking, Reed was going to get his ass kicked by a very tired Nova if he woke up the baby.

He started backing from the room, his eyes on his mate.

"If you're really asking me this time, yes, I want to marry you. I'll marry you."

His smile grew wide until his cheeks almost hurt. His animal was quiet, his heart was thumping like crazy in his chest, and he had this warm feeling running through his body. Joy. That's what he felt at that moment. Pure, unadulterated joy.

"I love you so much, Callie. As soon as everything calms down, we'll get married. Plan whatever kind you want. I don't care how much it costs. Anything you want. I saw a video once of these people releasing butterflies or some shit. You want that? We'll do it."

She clasped her hands in front of her face and smiled wide. "I love you, too. Now go to work and make enough money for my wedding dress," she teased as yet another horn blast echoed. "Go before he wakes up Rieka."

Micah stopped his retreat, hurried back across the room, and pressed his lips to hers in a passionate kiss, dipping his tongue into her mouth once, twice. He pulled back with a smile, then turned and hurried from the house.

He scowled at Reed—the asshole blaring his horn who was currently getting his ass chewed by Gray—and climbed into the passenger seat of his truck.

"Don't yell at me. I'm just trying not to get fired. Some of us want to keep our jobs," Reed complained, holding his hands out in front of him as Gray jabbed a finger in his face and said something about his daughter crying now.

Micah turned and looked back at Callie's house; she was standing in the doorway, wearing just her towel and smiling at him. He'd much rather she not stand there half-naked, but he loved that he got that image burned into his mind before he spent the afternoon separated from her. Fuck, she was so beautiful. And she was all his.

Reed rattled on the entire drive to the site, but Micah's mind was still back with Callie. He leaned his head against the rest and stared out the side window but he didn't see anything but the way his mate had looked when she'd pulled back that shower curtain, the way her body had felt against his that morning, the way she'd smiled all mushy when she'd said she'd marry him.

"I'm getting married," Micah blurted out, cutting off whatever stupid shit Reed was saying.

The cab of the truck was silent for a heartbeat, then Reed busted out laughing. "You asked her again?" he asked.

"Yep. This morning. She said yes."

"When?" Reed asked, turning to look at him for a second.

His smile was wide. For all the dude's ball busting, he was genuinely happy for Micah. He liked Callie. They all did. She'd fit in just as easily and quickly as Nova had. Well, Micah hadn't been exactly welcoming when Nova had shown up, but he'd just been trying to protect his Pack. And really, his own neck. Gray had been crazy possessive the moment she'd come onto their territory.

Micah rolled his head to look at Reed. "When all this bullshit is over. Told her to plan whatever kind she wants. I don't care if she wants to ride in on a fucking horse with a twelve-piece band playing in the background." He rolled his head back to look through the side window just as they pulled up to the site. "I wonder if Noah would hire me."

"Yeah, because if she ends up with that kind of wedding, your ass will definitely need a second job."

Gray and Tristan pulled beside them. They all grumbled as they trudged up the hill to start their day. At least it'd only be a half day. They would only have to be away from home for a few hours.

"This fucking sucks. I want to be home," Gray said, putting on his hard hat and climbing into an excavator.

Micah felt his pain. He'd only been away from Callie for just over twenty minutes and he already missed her. He could only imagine how bad it would be when they finally had kids.

And fuck, he couldn't wait to see her with the same round belly Nova'd had. He couldn't wait to see her cradling her belly and making a list of names.

For the next two hours, he thought of nothing but Callie and how she'd look in a white dress, how she'd look when they could finally live out their lives and plan their futures.

∞ ∞ ∞

Callie watched her man leave, pressing her lips to her palm and blowing him a kiss before he turned in his seat and the truck turned the corner and out of sight.

Hurrying back into the house, she pulled on a pair of shorts and a tank top, slipped her feet into some flip flops, then ran to get Emory. It was baby time without any interference from the guys. Emory was already making her way onto her porch before Callie got there.

"Had the same idea I did," Emory said with a smile. "I need some cuddling."

"Me, too."

They jogged to Nova's front door and tapped lightly.

Nova looked up and waved them in. She held Rieka to her chest, breastfeeding her. "You'll have to wait a few. She woke up starving. Let me rephrase that; she was starving when Reed's dumb butt woke her up."

"I was wondering what the hell he was thinking making all that noise," Emory said, taking a seat beside Nova. She stared down into

Rieka's face as she suckled from her momma. "She's more beautiful than she was yesterday."

"You've said that every day," Nova said, grinning at her friend.

"Well, it's true. She's just getting more beautiful every day. I figured Gray would've already put barbed wire up around the property."

Nova laughed softly, more of a snort as she tried to keep the noise down. "Trust me, he's already talking about all the crap he wants to do for security and how any boy who even thinks about talking to her will get his ass kicked."

Emory glanced up at Callie and there was sadness there. As happy as they all were that Nova had given birth to a daughter, there was still fear for her future. Even though the rules and laws were changing, she was still vulnerable in a time where a woman was subject to a man's claiming mark.

"Did you ever decide on a middle name?" Callie asked, trying to keep the sadness and worry out of her voice and off her face.

"Not yet. I can't think of anything pretty enough to go with Rieka," Nova said, pulling her bra cup up and fixing her shirt when the baby had her fill. She lifted her onto her shoulder and patted her back a few times until Rieka released an impressive belch. "Did she puke down my back again?"

Emory leaned back and shook her head. "All clean."

"What about your last name?" Callie asked.

"Rieka Aria Harvey?" Nova asked, her brows pulled together in thought. "That's kind of pretty, actually."

"That's how the Prides do it when a male claims a female. It's like combining the families, honoring them in a way. And not just the cubs. The females drop their middle names."

"Shame they're such dickwads, because that's kind of sweet," Emory said, holding her arms out as Nova offered Rieka to her.

"You mind watching her for a minute so I can take a shower?" Nova asked, standing before she even got an answer.

Emory never looked away from Rieka. "Take your time. We'll be fine. Won't we, Rie-rie," she said, cooing down at the baby.

"Oh lord. Here we go with the nicknames already," Nova said as she hurried to the bathroom and pulled the little sliding door in place. "I know you guys don't have any desire to see me naked, but it'd be nice to have a second to myself," she called through the door.

"Oh, honey. You can kiss alone time goodbye for the next eighteen years," Emory called back and then smiled down at Rieka. "She really is the most beautiful baby in the world. Aren't you?" she once again cooed.

Nova showered and rejoined them, offered them food or soda, then plopped back on the couch. "I don't think I've ever been this tired in my life," she said, closing her eyes as she rested her head against the back of the futon.

Their place was small like the rest of the houses, and now it looked even smaller with the bassinet and all the baby stuff everywhere. "Gray still want to build onto the place?" Callie asked, standing and reaching for Rieka when Emory offered her over.

"Yeah. He was talking to Micah about staying in his house while we work on this one," Nova said, never opening her eyes.

"Really?" Callie asked. Micah hadn't mentioned that to her.

Nova peeled one lid up. "Not like he ever stays in there anymore." Her smile widened and she lifted her head. "You seem like you're in a really good mood today. You get laid last night?"

Callie dipped her head as her cheeks grew hot. "This morning...and Micah asked me to marry him again."

"Wow. He's persistent," Emory said. "I still can't believe how different he is. He was always so...I don't know, cold and closed off."

"He's got a lot of history," Callie said, but wouldn't say anything more. That was his story to tell and she wouldn't betray his confidence like that.

"What did you say when he asked again?" Nova asked.

She smiled wide. "I said yes."

Nova clapped her hands together in excitement but winced when Rieka started hard. "Sorry, baby," she whispered to her daughter. "Mommy's just really excited. Oh, can she be your flower girl?"

"Duh," Callie said.

"When are you planning it for?" Emory asked.

With a shrug, Callie said, "I don't know. Probably when everything has blown over and we don't have to worry about whether Rhett, Brent, and the rest of Tammen will go all wedding crasher."

"Wait. How the hell would Rieka be her flower girl when she can't even crawl?" Emory asked.

"We'll pull her in a wagon or something," Nova said. "You going to go big?" She sat up further and pulled her feet under her, her eyes going to her daughter. She loved the look on Nova's face every time she looked at Rieka. It was a look full of love.

"I have no idea. I never thought about a wedding growing up. You know how it is for Shifters. Now, imagine not having any say in your future mate. Fantasizing about white gowns and flowers and stuff isn't something teenage lionesses do."

"Yeah, but now you can. You can have any kind of wedding you want. We should go get a bunch of bridal magazines," Nova said. "And by we, I mean you two because I'm not going to try lugging her in a car seat."

"Yeah, no. We're not supposed to leave. I'll just text Reed and tell him to grab a bunch," Emory said, pulling her phone from her back pocket.

"I wish I was there when he reads that text," Nova said with a giggle. "Can you picture his whining?" she said.

"Dude, why do they think I'm a chick?" Emory said, deepening her voice to imitate Reed.

"I actually thought he was gay when we first met," Nova admitted.

"I can see that," Callie said, rocking Rieka when she made a noise. She wasn't exactly fussing, but Callie was already nervous she'd done something wrong to irritate the tiny girl.

Rieka's little cheeks were round and pink, her hair dark like her momma's, and she definitely had Gray's nose. It was like she had the best of both parents. Emory was right; she was the most beautiful baby ever.

Rieka's eyes opened and seemed to focus on Callie a half second before she opened her mouth and let out a mewling sound. Then she squirmed and Callie looked up at Nova in a panic.

"She's fine. Just really waking up for a second. Don't worry; she'll go back to sleep so she can wake up in the middle of the night for real." Nova punctuated her sentence with a yawn. "I swear she wakes up every freaking hour. I'm surprised she hasn't woken any of you up yet." She tugged at her bra through her shirt. "My boobs are so sore already and she's only three days old. How do some women breastfeed for two freaking years?"

Emory snorted and crinkled her nose. "I've got to be honest, I've never really wanted kids. I'm glad you have one and I plan on spending the rest of her life spoiling the crap out of her, but not much of the rest sounds too appealing to me."

"Really?" Callie asked. She'd always wanted a family, but hated how that would come about. Now that her life was so different, she couldn't wait until Micah and she could start planning a family. She wanted at least six cubs. She had no idea if Micah was on board with so many, but they had the rest of their lives to discuss that. "I've always wanted to be a mom."

"I never really thought much about it before I met Gray. Yeah, I know it's only been three days, but I love being a mom so much. I didn't know it was possible to love someone so much." Her eyes did that soft loving thing again as she gazed at her daughter across the room.

Rieka's little arms shot into the air and she made another sound. Her eyes were wider now as she looked up at Callie, almost like she was confused as to who was holding her. Her body tensed and she released a long howl.

Callie stood immediately and carried her to Nova and deposited her into her mother's arms. Nope. She wanted to be a mom someday but she was not prepared for a crying baby.

The hair on the back of Callie's neck stood even as Rieka quieted. Why was she still stressed?

Turning toward the door, her body seemed to hum with energy and the hair was now rising all over her body. Emory stood slowly and a low growl trickled from her mouth.

Oh shit.

"Call Gray now!" Callie said, rushing to the door and locking it as she squinted and tried to see to the tree line. There was movement there, but she couldn't make out anything specific. Maybe it was just a deer, but she doubted it. There was no way her inner animal would react like this to anything but another predator.

"Where's Alan?" Emory said as she held the phone to her ear and waited. "Gray. Get home now…I don't know, but something's up…she's fine right now, but get your asses home." She ended the call and immediately made another.

Nova held Rieka tightly to her chest and yelled for Alan. He was on the porch in seconds, wiggling the doorknob. Callie unlocked it, let him in, and relocked it, her eyes on the woods the whole time.

"Colton, something's up. Can you…okay, yeah. See you soon." Emory shoved her phone back into her pocket and went to stand next to Callie. "Blackwater and Ravenwood are on their way, too," she said, moving to the other window and gripping the windowsill.

"They had to have been out there waiting for the guys to leave," Alan said, standing in front of his daughter and granddaughter as if ready to block anyone from getting to them. "How else would they know you were alone?"

Callie's heart stuttered when a flash of gold moved along the trees. And then another. They were here. The lions were here. And it was just the three women and Alan with the baby. The cowards had come when it was just the women. Of course, they had. They knew the Pack wouldn't stand by while the Pride attacked. They knew, even though Big River was outnumbered, it would be the fight of their lifetime.

"Fuck," Callie muttered, then looked over her shoulder at Nova. "Sorry," she said for cursing in front of the baby.

"No. That's an appropriate reaction. She might as well learn that now," Nova said in her usual light manner, but her eyes were wide, her face was pale, and she clutched Rieka protectively to her chest.

"What should we do?" Emory asked.

"Wait as long as we can and pray that someone else gets here before they decide to attack," Callie said, trying her damnedest to remain calm.

"And if they don't get here in time?" Emory asked, taking a step back away from the window.

"Then we Shift and fight back. They don't get near this fucking house," Callie said, anger building deep inside of her until she felt like she was on fire.

"Shit. Shit, shit, shit," Emory muttered over and over again.

Callie knew what was going through her mind; it was the same thing going through Callie's. They had to protect Rieka and Nova while trying to stay alive and out of the paws of the Pride. And it was just the two of them. Because she didn't want Alan to rush out to help. She wanted him inside as the last line of defense for his family.

With absolute horror, she watched as one massive male lion after another slowly stepped from the trees and into the sun. And behind them were four lionesses. From here, she couldn't tell which ones, but she'd bet her claws it was the same females who'd hand over their own offspring for a taste of power. They liked the laws, liked the hierarchy, and were loyal to Rhett. Then again, they were his mates, so why wouldn't they be loyal to him?

Four men in human form walked with the lions: Rhett, Brent, Trever, and Eli. Emory sucked in a sharp gasp when Eli came into view. "That mother fucker better keep his word," she whispered against the glass.

He might not fight against them, but Callie hoped he was serious when he'd said he'd try to keep the girls as safe as possible. But how could he do that without making himself out as a traitor to his Alpha?

Rhett led the Pride across the large open field, his eyes on Nova's house. He knew exactly where they were all hiding; his eyes were set on Callie even from that distance.

"Come on out, pussy cat," Rhett called. "Your mate is ready for you to come home."

Callie bit her lip to hold in her retort. It didn't matter how many times he or Brent claimed otherwise, Micah was her mate. Instead of responding, she took a step away from the door and hoped she was hidden in the shadows a little, hoped the sun in their eyes would keep them from seeing inside clearly.

"Either come out or the rest of them die," Brent bellowed, his tone angry where Rhett's was annoyed. "I promise I'll let the baby wolf live if you just come out now."

"Fuck," Callie said, a sob breaking through her lips. She looked back at Nova who was shaking her head.

"They're coming," Nova whispered. "Just hold on."

"Yeah, but so are they," Callie said, jerking her head toward the front door. There was no way her Pack would get there in time if Rhett decided to attack now. They were only about twenty yards away now and could close the space in seconds if they Shifted, too.

Turning to Emory, she shook her head. Emory was taking shallow gasps of air, her eyes wide. Callie felt the same panicked feeling.

Maybe she could just distract them. Hold them off long enough for at least someone from Blackwater to get to them. She'd just go out there and try to talk them down and Shift if she had to fight. She just hoped they'd keep it fair instead of all of them attacking her at once, or at least hoped Eli would keep his word and keep them from either killing her or stealing her.

"What are you doing?" Alan asked, taking a step forward and wrapping his hand around Callie's bicep, tugging her back a little.

"I'm going to try to buy us some time," Callie said.

Alan released her, but didn't step away. "Just stay in here. I'll go out."

"Yeah, right. They'll kill you, too," Callie said. "They don't want me dead. If…" She took a deep breath. "If they get me away before the guys get here, keep Micah calm. I trust you guys. I know you'll find me, but don't let his animal go rogue. Promise me," she said, looking to each of them.

"Please just stay inside," Emory begged, her eyes swimming with tears.

Callie looked outside again; they were ten yards away and still coming. With a slow shake of her head, she looked back at Emory. "I can't, Em. I can't let them hurt Rie."

"Really? Another nickname?" Nova said, but a tear had streaked down her cheek.

"I'll be fine." She hoped. "Stay in here. Lock the door. Make sure someone's coming."

"Please," Emory begged again, her unshed tears escaping and rolling off her chin.

With a forced smile, Callie smiled at her friends. "I'll be fine," she repeated, trying to convince them and herself.

With a steadying deep breath, she yanked the door open and stepped onto the porch. Before she could lose her courage, she descended the chairs and stomped forward and to her left, guiding them and their attention away from Nova's.

"Well, that was easier than I thought," Rhett said with a cruel smile. "You realize as punishment for your crimes, you'll be forced to begin breeding immediately," he said. Brent smiled wide at her as if he was already picturing all the ways he was going to hurt her.

Racking her brain for anything she could to keep them talking, she smiled back. "Hate to burst your bubble, but Micah already burst mine." Shit. That probably wasn't the best way to keep them calm and away from her, but it was the first thing that came to mind.

Brent stopped in his tracks and his eyes flashed bright gold. "You were mine to break," he growled out.

"Sorry. Not sorry." She smiled wider. This was a little more fun than she'd thought it would be. After all the years of mental abuse, it was kind of fun to taunt him, to throw back the same cruelty he'd shown her. "I'm not your mate, Brent. Don't you want to find your true mate? Don't you want to find love and happiness?"

Three of the guys snorted and Rhett rolled his eyes. "You've been hanging around the author too long. Did you read all her books and sigh like a little girl, picturing yourself in those stories? That shit ain't real, Callie. Love don't exist."

"It does. You guys, this isn't the way it has to be. Just because our parents forced it on us doesn't mean we have to keep doing it this way. Can you honestly say you're happy?"

A few more male lions stepped from the trees, their heads down, their eyes on Callie. It was terrifying to have the attention of so many dominant animals, but it was better their attention was on her than Nova, Emory, or Rieka.

The lionesses at Rhett's back looked up to the Alpha and waited. Was that hesitation in their eyes? Confusion, maybe? Could her words possibly have been getting through to them?

Rhett turned and looked at his harem. The lionesses turned back to her and hissed. Nope. Guess not. They were just waiting for their orders of whether or not to attack.

Attack *who* was what she was terrified to know. She didn't want to die. She wanted to live with Micah. She wanted that wedding he'd talked about. She wanted to have babies with him and then, someday, fifteen grandbabies. But she'd rather die here and now in this field than watch these assholes hurt her friends. She'd rather lay down in front of them, belly up, than have them anywhere near Rieka.

"Last chance, pussy cat," Rhett said. Something rustled behind her and she whirled. There were two male lions emerging from the trees just behind her house. She was surrounded. Worse. They were surrounding any escape for Nova and the baby.

"What are you doing?" Callie cried out as the lions glared at her and stalked closer to Nova and the baby.

Emory stepped onto the porch, fully naked. Guess talking time was over. It was time to fight.

As Emory trembled and her body broke and reshaped into a big white wolf, Callie turned back to the men who were still walking toward her without slowing. They wouldn't be talked down. There would be no negotiating, no persuading them to follow a different path.

Without wasting time removing her clothes, Callie reached down deep and gave her animal her body and prayed she could hold them off long enough for someone to get Nova and Rieka out of there before it was too late.

Brent smiled at her, more of a smirk, and Shifted into his massive lion and barreled for her. She hissed and crouched low the same time a truck bounced and skidded onto the dirt. The door opened and a second later, a gigantic bear was charging. Well, at least they had one more in the fight.

She wanted to tell Colton to change direction, to cut off the lions who were too close to Nova's house now. Emory stood at the top of the stairs in her wolf form, her lips peeled back from her teeth as she snarled and growled.

Just before Brent's body made contact with Callie, she had a moment of relief when the sounds of several other pickup trucks hit her sensitive ears.

But when the pain worked its way from her ribs to her brain, she just wondered if they'd made it on time.

∞ ∞ ∞

One phone call and Micah felt like his entire world had turned to black and white dipped in red. He couldn't focus on anything but the fear on Gray's face when he'd answered that call. They were in trouble. Their mates were in trouble. The lions were there.

Gray said Emory's call was vague, that something was wrong, but Micah knew deep in his gut that the fucking Pride had waited until the guys had gone to work to go after their women. Rhett had known they were unprotected, that the women's attention would solely be on the safety of the baby and would be easy prey.

And now, all he could do was sit in Reed's fucking truck and pray that they'd get there on time. Reed was on the phone, but Micah couldn't make out the words through the blood rushing through his ears.

"Dude, did you hear me? Colton is almost there and the rest of Blackwater and Ravenwood are on the way. Aron said he'd received a call that Deathport is on their way, too."

"A call from who?" Micah growled out, his animal right there, watching and waiting for the chance to kill anyone who dared come near his mate.

"He didn't know. Some dude. Wouldn't tell him his name and the call was blocked. Said Deathport is on their way to join those fuckers."

Son of a bitch. This was something they'd all feared from the very beginning. But there had been this tiniest glimmer of hope somewhere inside of Micah where he'd thought maybe Deathport would stay out of it. Yeah, they still wanted Emory, but they also knew Big River would take out anyone who harmed their family. It was a big ass risk.

Once Brent and Rhett were out of the picture, Micah made a promise to the universe to get Anson's ass out of the fucking picture, too. He'd been nothing but trouble for Big River since the day Emory and Tristan had joined them. It was time for him to go away. Permanently.

Gray was in front of them, his truck flying down the highway as they passed car after car, weaving in and out of traffic. Luckily, they didn't pass any cops and avoided smashing into anyone when they ran a red light.

And then they were on the first leg of their long driveway. He'd always loved living out in the middle of nowhere, the isolation and quiet their property offered. But now that there was the biggest emergency of their lives, Micah cursed how far they'd had to drive to get home.

When Reed's truck turned the corner and their homes came into view, Micah couldn't make sense of what he was seeing. It was chaos and looked like a movie playing out right in front of him.

There were wolves, lions, bears, and panthers battling. There were lions and wolves lying prone in the dirt, but Micah could tell from where they were the wolves didn't belong to anyone in his Pack.

Before they were even close enough, Micah lunged from the car and was Shifting as he ran. Callie. Where was Callie? There were lionesses fighting, but three of them were locked on a big brown grizzly bear.

His paws hit the ground hard, his claws digging into the mud and grass, his eyes darting everywhere as he tried to make sense of this horror, as he tried to find his mate. Would he know her from the other lionesses?

His wolf lifted his snout and howled long and loud. He knew without a doubt both he and his wolf would know Callie from anywhere.

There. She was swiping her paws at two male lions and he'd put fucking money down at least one of them was Brent. Reed was racing beside him now as Gray and Tristan ran in wolf form toward Gray's house.

Nova was nowhere in sight, so Micah hoped she was inside safe with her baby. Alan charged a lion who stepped onto the bottom step the same time Gray hit him from the back side. Turning his attention back to Callie, he barely missed Anson as he dove at him.

Sliding to a stop as Anson and Felix cut off his path, he dove at Anson, his mouth open, and clamped down on his shoulder.

Shit. There were two of them on Micah, but he wasn't afraid for himself. He just feared they were slowing him from getting to Callie in time.

A blur of black fur streaked past and Felix was knocked away. Aron swiped his claws at Felix and caught his hind leg. Felix yelped in pain but turned on Aron.

Anson was on his feet still, even as Micah held on with everything he had. Micah shook his head and tried to knock Anson off balance, but he twisted and snapped his teeth.

A loud roar broke through the rest of the sounds of battle and made Micah's stomach clench. It was a battle cry. A war cry. It was Colton.

Anson's body was yanked from Micah's teeth and tossed a few hundred feet and landed with a hard thud. He stood, wobbled, collapsed. But he wasn't dead. Not yet.

Leaving Anson for Colton, Micah turned back toward Callie and weaved through the various fights. They were definitely outnumbered, even with the other groups' help. But where Tammen and Deathport fought for sick reasons, his people, his friends and family fought for love, for justice, and for revenge.

Callie was on the back of a wolf, her claws dug deep in his back, her teeth clamped around the back of its neck as a constant growl vibrated from her chest. The wolf shook and scrambled, trying to get her off, but she just held on.

I'm coming, Callie. Hold on.

The wide back and dark mane of a male lion blocked his view of his mate. He was charging Callie. Fuck no. Not happening. Pulling from deep inside, Micah pushed harder until he was slamming into the hind quarters of the lion. The fucker was bigger than Micah, but only by inches. And Micah had a fucked up hybrid animal. A *possessive*, fucked up hybrid animal. And this son of a bitch was signing his own death certificate by daring to touch what was his.

The lion chuffed out a short roar and shook his mane. Micah ducked his head and snarled, baring his teeth as he stalked Brent. And he knew without a doubt this fucker was definitely the male who'd tried to force himself on Callie. Even in his animal form, Micah could feel the same twisted evil radiating from him.

Callie was beside him now, her ears flat to her head, her canines bared, a hiss pouring from her. She was so fucking beautifully fierce.

Brent swiped a massive paw at them both, but they ducked out of the way. Micah lunged at him, but jumped back when Brent swiped a paw again. And then a lioness joined his side, her eyes bouncing between Micah and Callie, probably trying to decide which one she should go after.

She'd made her decision. She jumped at Callie even as Callie tried to bat her away, and they tumbled to the ground. Brent took Micah's moment of distraction and attacked. And then his mouth was around Micah's throat.

He kicked with all four paws, but Brent's teeth were digging through his fur and puncturing his flesh. Rolling his eyes to the side, Micah inwardly smiled when he watched Callie chase the lioness off and trot to a stop, her head held high. At least he got to see that before he died in Brent's jaws.

Chapter Twelve

Callie swelled with a little pride as she watched the lioness tuck her tail and run away. *Take that, bitch.* All that time she'd been with them, that bitch had always acted like she was so much better than Callie. Than everyone else, really. So, when she'd bested her, when she'd drawn blood from her shoulder and chased her off, all she could do was gloat.

Until she turned back around and found Brent on top of her mate, his jaws clenched, blood welling on Micah's throat.

Peeling her lips back, she released a screech, the only warning Brent would get that he was about to die. How dare that asshole come here? How dare he threaten her family? How dare he try to steal away her happiness?

How dare that mother fucker touch her mate.

Callie jumped on Brent's back and latched on with her teeth and every claw she had. She bit and chewed and tore until he had to release Micah. He shook his big body, trying to dislodge her, but she was relentless. She had rage fueling her and her animal was just as pissed as she was. No way would she let someone like him win.

There was fur everywhere, bodies clashing, snarls and growls and howls filled the air. But Callie focused only on Brent. He rolled to the ground and tried to crush her under his weight, but she didn't let go, even as the air whooshed from her lungs from the impact. Movement caught her eye. Micah. He was bleeding but he was on his feet.

He shook his head as if trying to clear it then focused on where Callie lay squished under Brent's weight. They locked eyes and it was like they were able to communicate even in this form.

Micah dove for Brent's belly and slashed with his claws. Brent roared and rolled back to his feet, Callie still clinging to him like a leech. As Micah went for him again, Callie adjusted her grasp so she was now hanging onto his throat with her front paws, her claws digging into his fur and flesh.

Brent twisted his head and shook his body, but couldn't risk rolling onto her again. Micah and Callie worked as a team, one distracting while the other made another tear in his flesh. They were going to get their pound and then some.

Brent was stumbling now as lash after lash from the claws of Micah and Callie weakened him. The overwhelming scent of blood did something to Callie's animal. She was drunk from it. She was drowning in it and it seemed to come from every side.

Adjusting her weight again, she opened her mouth and clamped on lower until she knew she was mere inches from his jugular. With one of her paws, she grabbed at his face, clawing at where she guessed his eyes to be. He swatted his paws, trying to get her away from him, trying to save his eyes while trying to shake her off his throat.

He stumbled and went down. Micah lunged at him again and bit the other side of his throat. Callie locked eyes with Micah and tightened her jaw.

And then Brent was no longer struggling, no longer fighting, no longer trying to stand.

Releasing her hold on him, she backed away, her eyes on Brent in case this was some kind of ploy, and bumped Micah with her shoulder. He stepped back and they watched as Brent's chest rose and fell in shallow gasps. His eyes were on Callie, but they were unfocused. And then his pupils dilated, his chest stopped moving, and a long breath rattled from his chest.

He was dead. Brent was dead. He was no longer a threat to them. Holy shit.

Elation warred with guilt. She was free from him, but she'd killed someone. She'd taken a life. She could still taste his blood in her mouth as she stared down at his lifeless body.

She wanted to wallow in that guilt, but the battle was still going on around them, even if it had far less energy. There were bodies littering the grounds of their property, but as far as she could tell, it was none of her people.

Looking around to see if anyone needed help, Callie's heart almost stopped. Emory was on the far edge of their property, off to the right of their houses. She was being corralled by four wolves, and she snapped her teeth at them and snarled.

Without bothering to check to see if Micah was following, she darted off to join Emory's fight. Callie could tell what they were doing. They weren't trying to hurt or kill Emory. They were trying to get her away from her friends and family. Trying to split her up so they could take her away.

One wolf jumped forward while another circled around behind Emory. She no longer had an escape route. Callie couldn't seem to make her legs move fast enough.

A deep, bone rattling roar filled the air and a lion with a pitch-black mane charged the group of wolves. Eli. He was keeping his word. At least she hoped that was what he was doing.

As another wolf snapped at Emory, almost making contact with her shoulder, the lion plowed into him, knocking him away. Eli reared his head back, dropped it down quickly, and latched his teeth onto the back of Emory's neck. She yelped and howled in pain and tried to scrabble away, but Eli's grip was too strong.

That son of a bitch. He'd played them like fools.

But he didn't kill her. He didn't force her away with his big body. He released his hold on her neck and then stood in front of her, chuffing and growling at the wolves. They lowered their heads and ears, whined, and backed away, turning and trotting to join their friends.

What had just happened?

Callie didn't slow down. She kept running for her friend, for her new sister. Eli shook his mane out, threw his head back, and released another roar before walking away, his big paws hitting the ground almost silently.

Micah snapped his teeth at Eli as he passed, but the lion didn't spare him another glance and just kept walking toward the woods in the opposite direction.

Callie looked around; it was over. There were only a handful of lions and wolves left standing and they were retreating. Her friends had won. They'd won.

Shifting back into her human form, she checked the wound in her thigh; it wasn't too deep. It'd heal by morning with just a scar. A reminder of what had happened that day.

One by one, her family Shifted back and checked each other over.

"What the hell just happened?" Emory said, holding her hand over the puncture marks on her neck.

Callie turned Emory and lifted her hair. And then she gasped. "Oh my god, Emory. He marked you."

"What?!" Emory yelled, whipping around. "That son of a bitch."

Micah grimaced at the cuts and gashes all over his body. "I think he saved you from those wolves." He shook his head and looked to where the Pride and Pack had disappeared through the trees.

"Then why the hell did he mark me?" Emory asked with a quivering lip.

"Because then the wolves couldn't have you," Callie said softly, her eyes following Micah's gaze. "Holy crap."

Micah led Callie and Emory to join their family and friends. Everyone was battered and bleeding, but alive.

"Oh my god!" Nova cried out from her front porch. "Help!"

And then everyone was in motion again.

Alan lie in a heap on the other side of Nova's porch, a large gash across his abdomen steadily leaking blood. Callie watched in horror as Gray and Carter hurriedly tried to staunch the flow. Shifters could heal quickly, but they weren't immortal. A wound like that could be fatal if he lost too much blood. He was ashen and his eyes were unfocused as he stared up at the darkening sky. Had they been too late? How long had he laid like that?

Callie looked around at the bodies. Was it possible Rhett lie amongst those bodies? What about Trever? Did Colton get his revenge? And if Alan died, what then? Would there be more fighting?

She climbed the steps and reached for Nova, but pulled back. Callie was covered in blood, both hers and Brent's. She didn't want any of it on Nova or Rieka. They remained untainted and needed to stay that way.

And they were both safe. There wasn't a scratch on either of them.

"Come on, Dad. I just got you in my life. Don't you dare leave me, too," Nova said as tears ran nonstop down her face. Rieka lie silent in her arms as if she was aware of the moment, of how dire the situation was.

Micah wrapped an arm around Callie's shoulders and pulled her close, his lips on her temple as they watched the Alphas try to save Alan's life. So much death because of Tammen. She refused to blame herself ever again. She hadn't caused this. She'd just wanted to be free. To live her life the way she deserved. Tammen and others like them were who caused this disaster, caused all the blood on their property.

It would take weeks to get the stench of death away, probably just as long before the rain washed the blood away. They would have to bury the bodies of the fallen. They'd still give them an honorable burial, even if they had come to kill Big River. Even if they had come to destroy their lives one by one.

∞ ∞ ∞

Callie waited outside Reed's house, shifting her weight from one foot to the other. Micah leaned against the railing and smirked.

"You excited?" he asked, glancing behind him when the door opened.

"Duh," she said.

It was the first time she'd get out of the territory since the almost issue at the bar over a month ago. Even though she wasn't locked inside, she was getting cabin fever. Now that she'd tasted freedom, she wanted to go out in the world and experience everything.

They wouldn't experience everything tonight, but at least she'd get to drink a beer and dance. Nova stepped out with Rieka in her arms, Gray and Alan following close behind.

"Are you sure this is okay? I can stay behind," Nova said, handing the baby to her grandpa.

"No you can't," Gray said, kissing Rieka on the forehead and wrapping an arm around Nova's shoulders. "She'll be fine. You haven't left her side in weeks. It's time to get out."

"We'll be fine. I'm going to read to her and play with her and maybe give her a bunch of candy," Alan said, swaying the tiny girl in his arms.

Nova rolled her eyes. "Yeah. Ha ha. So funny. Just call me immediately if there're any problems. Or if you get tired. Or if she starts crying."

"Nova, I've been around a few babies. I'll be fine," Alan said before sadness washed through his eyes. But just as quickly as it'd come, it was gone.

He hadn't gotten to raise his own daughter, hadn't gotten to see Nova grow up, but he had a chance to make up for it with his granddaughter. Snuggling her close, he closed his eyes and inhaled deeply, breathing in her soft, powdery baby scent.

"Okay, but…okay. My phone is on me and it will be all night. I pumped enough bottles to feed an army and they're in the fridge. You know how to warm them, right?"

"Nova, he's fine. Let's go. Everyone's waiting," Gray said, trying to guide her away from the house and to his truck.

She sighed heavily, constantly looking back at where Alan waved goodbye. "Thanks, Dad. Love you. Love you, Rieka. Mommy will only be gone for a little while," she said, raising her voice the further away she walked.

Emory, Reed, and Tristan were already in Reed's truck waiting. They led the convoy down the driveway and into town. They were headed to Moe's for some food, beer, music, and friends. It was a belated celebration of their win. Not just *their* win. Everyone's win. They showed Tammen and others like them that they would no longer be able to imprison women without a fight. Other Packs, Clans, and even a few Prides in the surrounding areas offered their assistance should the situation arise again. It was nice to know they had backup if they ever needed it.

The radio was up in Micah's truck and Callie put her hand through the open window. She loved the feeling of the warm air rushing past her, and tilted her face toward the bright sun. They were quickly moving toward a balmy summer, but for now, she was enjoying being able to enjoy the fresh air.

"You're so beautiful," Micah said.

Callie lifted her head to find Micah alternating between watching the swatches of sun and shade wash over her face and the road in front of him.

"You're not so bad yourself," she said flirtatiously. Smiling at him, she turned back to the sun and closed her eyes.

Everything was perfect. Their life, while maybe not easy, was perfect. Alan had healed nicely. They hadn't heard a word from Tammen or Deathport since the fight. Brent, Rhett, Trever, and Anson were dead. And the council was working on the new laws, including whether or not an unmarked, unmated female was completely off-limits. When it was all through, any female would be able to walk away, even if she was mated, even if she was marked. She'd have the same freedom of choice as the human women.

And it had been because of her Pack. She refused to take credit for any of it. When she'd run from the Tammen Pride, all she'd had in mind was getting away and being free of Brent's cruelty. But her Pack, her friends from the Blackwater Clan and the Ravenwood Pride, had fought beside them, fought for female Shifters, fought for freedom.

Her heart was full and her life was complete.

There were several trucks and cars parked along the long, white bar, including a blue Mustang she was very familiar with. "Hey. Eli's here," Callie said, glancing over at Reed's truck to see if Emory noticed.

By her wide eyes and her hands flailing as she yelled in the cab of Reed's truck, she got her answer.

"Well, then. This should be interesting," Micah said, stepping from his seat and rounding the hood.

Callie pushed her door open and slipped her hand into Micah's, letting him help her down from his tall truck. "Please behave," she said, looking up at him with a cocked brow.

"I don't think I'm the one you have to worry about," he said, nodding at Emory, who was stomping toward the door.

"Emory!" Callie yelled, running to catch up to her. "Let's just have some fun. Pretend he's not even here."

Emory's nostrils flared with her angry breaths, her eyes were bright blue, and she trembled with the effort it took to control her animal. "If that asshole comes near me…"

"Then I'll move out of the way so you can kick him in the balls," Callie said. All four men cringed and involuntarily squeezed their legs together.

"There's no reason for all that," Reed said. "Couldn't you just punch him in the nose or something." His hand cupped his junk as Gray yanked the door open.

"Nope. I'm going to ram my knee right into his balls if he even looks like he plans to talk to me," Emory said, filing in behind Gray and Nova.

Reed groaned and grumbled as he stepped in behind Tristan. "Why can't we just have one normal night?"

"Since when could normal and Big River ever be used in the same sentence?" Callie asked, tipping her head back when Micah bent forward for a quick peck on her lips. He smiled against her lips, then held the door open for her to step in.

The room was dimly lit as usual, but there was so much noise, laughter, deep voices talking, pool balls clicking against each other, even music playing low in the background. It was the sounds of life. They were the sounds of not being grounded to the Big River territory.

Her heart immediately began to flutter but for a completely different reason. With the exception of a few guys in there, these were her people, her friends, her family. And she loved every single one of them.

As Noah pulled a few tables together and Gray, Tristan, and Colton grabbed a few more chairs, Callie looked around the room. Eli was, indeed, there. He sat with a few male lions she'd met in passing but who'd never really given her many problems. At their table sat Kaleb and Barrett from Deathport. Who were the Alphas of those groups now? Was Eli in charge of Tammen? He'd said he didn't want that rank, that he had no desire to be Alpha, but did he have a choice?

All the members of Tammen and Deathport had fought against them, but she also knew an Alpha's orders couldn't be ignored. They'd been unwilling participants in a war that wasn't theirs. One they didn't want.

Felix was there, too. He glared at Big River but didn't say a word. Probably best for him. He no longer had a slew of allies like he did before. And just because the war was over didn't mean every single one of her friends wouldn't stomp his ass into the ground just because he'd been one of Rhett's biggest supporters in his efforts at blackmailing Emory into their Pack.

"Yeah, keep staring, asshole," Micah said when he followed Callie's gaze to Felix.

Felix lifted his lip in a sneer, but looked away. Good choice.

Micah continued to glare in Felix's direction long after the wolf had averted his eyes. Callie laid her hand on Micah's knee under the table and squeezed. "Want me to kick him in the balls?" she teased.

That same cringy look came over his face and he wrinkled his nose and shook his head. "No ball smashing tonight," he said, bumping her shoulder with his.

Noah came to their table with a large circular tray filled with shot glasses. Once everyone had one, he stood at the end of the table, raised his glass, and smiled wide. "To family," he called out.

"To family," they all repeated before tapping the bottom of the glass on the table and tossing the drink back.

The second the booze hit the back of Callie's throat, her eyes watered and she twisted up her face. It burned a path down her throat and into her stomach.

"No girly drinks tonight," Reed said, setting his glass on the table top.

"Dude, that was like straight kerosene," Emory said, her eyes squinted, her lips pursed, and her nose wrinkled.

"Just a little whiskey to put some hair on your chest," Noah said, picking up the tray and heading back to the bar.

"Yeah, I'd rather not have hair on my chest," Emory said, grabbing Colton's beer and taking a long pull from it to wash out her mouth.

"Hey, sure. You can have some of my beer," Colton said with a wink.

Gray and Micah stood and helped Noah carry over a few buckets of beer. She watched the way Micah's ass moved in his jeans, but movement across the bar caught Callie's eye.

Eli was standing, his eyes on their table. Shit. Maybe there *would* be some ball smashing tonight, after all. His eyes were on Emory as he slowly made his way over, his hands in view as if he wanted to make sure they all knew he wasn't a threat.

"What the fuck do you want?" Colton asked, turning in his seat to see what the girls were looking at.

Reed, Tristan, Carter, and Luke all stood and raised their heads, looking at him down their noses. There was so much dominance, power, and anger wafting from her table it was dizzying.

"To say sorry," Eli said in his deep rumbling voice.

"You said it. Bye," Colton said, never bothering to rise from his seat. He was the one closest to Eli. It wouldn't take much energy for the big bear to lunge at Eli's throat.

"I'm sorry for what happened, I'm sorry I couldn't stop Rhett, and I'm sorry for..." His eyes dropped to the ground and he took a deep breath. "I'm sorry for marking you. I didn't know what else to do," he said to Emory. "I saw the wolves. It was the first thing on my lion's mind."

"I'm sure it was," Nova said, her arms crossed over her chest as she narrowed her eyes at him.

"No. That's not what I meant. I had to stop them. They kept trying to bite her. I didn't want them to mark her. They were trying to claim her."

"Yeah," Emory whispered, her eyes wide and her lips parted as she sucked in shallow pants of air.

"I don't want anything from you. You're still free. I never wanted anything more from you. I just didn't want them to hurt you." He dipped his head at her, turned, and walked out the door, leaving them all gaping after him.

And then all eyes darted to Emory. She was staring at the closed door, her eyes still wide, but now her hand was covering the mark on the back of her neck.

Memories of the day Brent had found Callie at the bar played themselves over and over in her head. Memories of how Emory had reacted when Eli had appeared, the way she'd watched the door even after he'd disappeared through it, the way Eli watched her every time they were near each other.

There was way more there than the lion marking Emory for her protection.

But that was for them to figure out. Tonight? Tonight was a celebration of life.

"You okay?" Callie whispered when the conversation started back up and the guys started passing around beers.

"Yeah," Emory said, shaking her head and blinking rapidly a few times. "Yeah, I'm fine. Just didn't want to talk to him," she said.

Nova and Callie stared at Emory. It was Nova who spoke up. "It's okay if you want to go talk to him. We'll go with you if you're scared."

"Why the hell would I want to talk to him?" Emory asked, her dark brows furrowing.

"Em—"

"Nope. Not going there, Nova. This isn't some novel. Just let it go." Emory picked up her bottle and took a swig, indicating she was done with the subject of the lion Shifter and his saving mark.

"So, if he marked you, does that mean you're mated to a lion? Are you now part of his harem?" Leave it to Reed to bring up the very subject Emory was trying to squash.

"We're not mated. I'm not mated to anyone. And sure as hell not a fucking lion," she said, but Callie didn't miss the way her eyes glistened when she looked down and pretended to rifle through her purse.

Later. Later, Callie and Nova would prod further, try to dive into this a little more. Hoping to help Emory save face, Callie redirected the spotlight.

"We're getting married," she announced.

Micah smiled wide and draped his arm around her shoulders, beaming with pride and joy.

"No shit?" Colton said.

"No shit," Micah said.

"That's fucking awesome. Noah! More shots! Our girl finally said yes," Colton said, waving his hand at Noah.

Their girl. And she was. She was theirs. She belonged here. She belonged with these people. Maybe she was the only lion in the Pack, but that didn't seem to matter to any of them. They'd never treated her like an outcast. Had never treated her like she didn't belong. When they Shifted for a hunt, they just expected her to come along, even if she was the only one able to climb lower trees and tended to be faster than the wolves.

"When?" Noah asked when he came back with another round of shots.

"Nova informed me we're having an early fall wedding," Callie said, winking over at Nova.

"Hey! We can't have the same damn wedding anniversary. I want all the attention on me."

"Are you going to have a big one?" Carter asked.

Callie shrugged and looked up at Micah. "Don't know. Haven't really decided yet. But you're all invited."

"I want to be the best man," Reed said, his hand shooting into the air like a school child.

Micah snorted and rolled his eyes. "I'm not sure you're even invited," he said with the beer bottle to his lips.

"Everyone's invited," Callie said, poking Micah with her elbow.

He made an *oomph* sound and pulled the bottle away before spilled it everywhere.

"*Everyone*," she repeated, smiling at Micah. "Hey. Should we invite the council?"

"You did say everyone," Nova teased. "I swear I'm already buzzed."

"You haven't had any alcohol in over ten months. And you're already a light weight. Might want to pace yourself, baby," Gray said.

"Or you could always pick a fight again," Reed said.

The group laughed and teased. They joked and told stories. It was normal. So maybe that word and Big River could be used in the same sentence. For tonight.

∞ ∞ ∞

Eli sat in his Mustang and stared at the bar. He should go back in. He should tell Emory everything. He should tell her what he'd known since the day he'd seen her the night they'd followed Callie onto Big River territory.

But he wouldn't.

He started the engine and aimed his car toward Tammen territory. He'd known she'd be there tonight. He'd heard through the gossip mill Big River and their friends were finally going into public to celebrate their win against his Pride.

Nah. Not really his Pride. They'd won against Rhett. Against Brent. Against mother fuckers like them. He'd never wanted any part of it but had never had any choice.

The Pride was quiet now, and the mood was different. The females who'd survived the attack on Big River were angry. Those who'd been brought here against their will celebrated silently. They were free. But they still hadn't left.

They had nowhere else to go.

Their own Prides, their own families had sold them off, given them away. They were stuck with Tammen until they were able to make their own paths. But Eli was the Alpha now, even though he really didn't want that role. He'd made sure the woman had the choice of whether they stayed in the house with the male they'd been sold to or lived with other females.

There were a few men who were pissed at him for that decision, but for the most part, the new rules were accepted. The new laws hadn't been put in place by the council yet, but he'd been ready for a change years ago.

"Hey," Luna called out when he stepped from his car.

His sister was so much happier these days. Then again, who wouldn't be? Her chosen male was dead. He couldn't hurt her anymore. Her bruises had healed up long ago, but the scar on the back of her neck and across her cheek would always be there, the silver line and punctures stark against her tanned skin.

"Where were you?" she asked, walking with him into his house.

He'd housed females in his house, but none had ever been a part of some fucked up harem. Even now, Luna and two other females stayed there, taking up three of the rooms while he slept on the couch.

"Moe's."

"Was she there?" she asked, leaning against the counter as he pulled a beer from the fridge.

"Who?" he asked, keeping his back to her. He'd never been good at lying and she'd see the fib in his eyes.

"Oh, come on. I'm not stupid, Elijah. Essie told me all about the female you marked."

"I was just trying to protect her," he said, finally turning to look at her.

She was so much different than he was. Where Eli was tall with black hair, darker golden-brown eyes, and tattoos from his fingertips to his collarbone, Luna was petite, standing around six inches shorter than his six-foot-two, and had pale blonde hair. Her eyes were more of a honey color and her skin was void of any marks other than scars. She'd always said she had enough permanent art. She didn't need to add any color.

"Tell her how you feel, Elijah. Who knows, maybe she feels the same way."

Luna hugged him around his waist, grabbed his bottle of beer, and walked away with it.

If Luna had come to that conclusion, what was the chance everyone else in the Pride saw the same thing?

Didn't matter. She hated him. Her entire Pack hated him. And he didn't blame them.

That night, he laid in bed and thought about the moment his lion had claimed her. He'd been battling his animal over Emory for months, and then he'd lost control.

And now, he was a male without his mate. And his lion was quickly losing its fucking mind.

∞ ∞ ∞

Callie handed a hammer up to Gray who was trying to balance a board in place. The Pack and Clan had been working on making Gray and Nova's house bigger for four weeks. And it was almost done. They'd built an extra room on the back and another loft up top so there would be some semblance of privacy as little Rieka got older.

"You guys think you'll have any more?" Callie asked Nova, who was holding the boards below her.

"Not anytime soon. Or ever. That little girl never sleeps, I swear," she said. All eyes went to Rieka, who was flailing her arms and kicking her legs in her little playpen a few feet away. Alan sat nearby, ready to tend to her if she fussed.

Alan had ended up buying a little place similar to Callie's, but the additions were put on hold until they finished Nova's house. He was content staying with Reed, although Reed liked to pretend he needed his bachelor pad *in case he brought home any chicks*. His words.

They'd all laughed at him since the guy had zero game when it came to flirting. He tended to open his mouth and spew out the first thought that came to mind. While Callie found it endearing, it usually scared off any potential dates.

"What about you guys?" Emory asked as she lounged in a chair near Rieka.

"I keep asking her the same thing," Micah said from the rooftop.

Callie smiled up at him and shook her head. "And like I keep saying, I want to enjoy us before we add any babies. Besides, do you have any idea how hard it is to carry cubs?"

"Cubs?"

"Uh, yeah. Lionesses tend to carry more than one at a time," Callie said with a shiver.

"What if they're wolves?" Emory asked.

"Or coyotes?" Micah said from the roof.

Callie's wide eyes flew up to his. Holy crap. He'd just said that in front of everyone.

When Nova and Emory looked at her with matching confused frowns, Callie shrugged.

"Yeah, I'm part coyote. Deal with it," Micah said, turning his back on everyone.

And then literally every single person was looking at her with wide eyes as if she'd finish the story. She laughed nervously and sucked her lips into her mouth. No way was she telling them everything. That was for Micah to disclose. Hell, that was a lot of information for one day.

After a few minutes, they all seemed to regain their composure. "That definitely explains a lot," Nova said, handing a board up to Gray. "Now I know why you're always so grumpy. I would be, too, if my animal was that confused."

Micah looked over the edge and growled at Nova, but there was a small smile on his lips and zero conviction behind the sound.

Two hours later, the house was done and they all stood back, staring at their work. The Blackwater Clan had showed up toward the end, but they'd put in enough work over the last few weeks. They'd come for the meat.

"Who's grilling?" Colton asked as he carried over bags of food. "I bought. You cook."

Callie stood off to the side watching everyone, watching as they carried the food to the grill, as they situated the chairs in a perfect circle.

"You look happy," Micah said in her ear as his arms wrapped around her from behind.

"I am." She turned and threw her arms around his neck. "You did this. You gave this to me."

He shook his head slowly, his eyes on her lips. "No. This was all you. You saved yourself. You fought for yourself. You brought joy into our lives. You brought joy into my life."

He kissed her and she held his head there, savoring his taste. "I love you, Micah. I always will."

"I love you, too, mate. Always."

Character Index

Big River Pack
Grayson (Gray) Harvey – Alpha – wolf
Micah – Second – wolf
Reed – wolf
Tristan – wolf
Emory – wolf
Nova – wolf – mate to Gray

Blackwater Clan
Carter – Alpha – bear
Colton – bear
Luke – bear
Noah – bear – owner of Moe's Tavern

Ravenwood Pride
Aron – Alpha – panther
Mason – panther
Brax – panther – brother to Daxon
Daxon – panther – brother to Brax

Deathport Pack
Anson – Alpha – wolf
Felix – Second – wolf
Barrett – wolf
Kaleb – wolf
Tanner – wolf

Tammen Pride
Rhett – Alpha – lion
Trever – lion
Elijah (Eli) – lion
Brent – lion
Callie Taylor – lioness

Council Members
Alan Price – wolf - Nova's biological dad
Frank – wolf – Colton's dad

Made in the USA
Monee, IL
26 July 2025